He could s... from her eyes even as she squee... them shut, her shoulders juddering as she gave in to her feelings.

And Theo was torn between his duty and her distress. Torn between admiration that a naive princess had eluded discovery for so long and frustration that she refused to accept what her discovery meant. Torn between respect for the fight in this pint-size princess and desire. Desire that had been building from the moment Theo had captured her in his arms and felt the heat triggered between them and smelled her citrusy scent.

Because she was wrong about one thing. She wasn't worth nothing in his eyes. She was worth so much more than that. But she was still a princess. He had no right to have feelings for her. He wasn't entitled to feel anything for her. She was a case. She was a rescue.

But she was also a woman.

USA TODAY bestselling author **Trish Morey** just loves happy endings. Now that her four heroines-in-training have grown up and flown the nest, Trish is enjoying her own happy ending—the one where you downsize, end up living in an idyllic coastal region with the guy you married and, better still, realize you still love each other. There's a happy-ever-after right there. Or a happy new beginning!

Trish loves to hear from her readers—you can email her at trish@trishmorey.com.

Books by Trish Morey

Harlequin Presents

Bartering Her Innocence
A Price Worth Paying?
Consequence of the Greek's Revenge
Prince's Virgin in Venice
After-Hours Proposal

21st Century Bosses

Fiancée for One Night

Bound by His Ring

Secrets of Castillo del Arco

Visit the Author Profile page
at Harlequin.com for more titles.

GREEK'S ROYAL RUNAWAY

TRISH MOREY

PRESENTS

MIX
Paper | Supporting responsible forestry
FSC® C021394
FSC
www.fsc.org

Harlequin® PRESENTS™

PLEASE RECYCLE · THIS PRODUCT IS RECYCLABLE ·

Recycling programs for this product may not exist in your area.

ISBN-13: 978-1-335-21354-9

Greek's Royal Runaway

Copyright © 2026 by Trish Morey

Harlequin Enterprises ULC
22 Adelaide St. West, 41st Floor
Toronto, Ontario M5H 4E3, Canada
www.Harlequin.com

HarperCollins Publishers
Macken House, 39/40 Mayor Street Upper,
Dublin 1, D01 C9W8, Ireland
www.HarperCollins.com

Printed in Lithuania

GREEK'S
ROYAL RUNAWAY

To the magical Lord Howe Island, one of the most glorious places in the world. If you haven't been lucky enough to visit yourself, I hope this story gives you a glimpse of the paradise that is Lord Howe.

PROLOGUE

Two hours out of Sydney the small jet banked, jolting Theo Mylonakos' attention from the photographs he was studying. He looked out the window, his gaze snared by the tiny speck of emerald amidst the sea of sparkling sapphire.

Lord Howe Island.

Tropical islands ordinarily held no attraction for him, but this one was different. His eyes narrowed as the plane grew closer, taking in the way the island cradled a coral-fringed bay, the twin mountains at one end looming so high over the peaks at the other, one might wonder why the weight didn't send the island toppling over and spinning to the bottom of the ocean.

And somewhere down there, pretending to be an everyday nobody rather than a member of one of Europe's oldest royal families, his quarry was hiding, Princess Isabella d'Montcroix, no doubt congratulating herself that she'd managed to evade those looking for her for the best part of six weeks.

Her brother, Prince Rafael, had led them to believe that the Princess was simply that—a typical twenty-something princess. Refined. Demure. *Innocent*. And when he looked at the photographs of the pretty hazel-eyed blonde, he'd believed what he'd been told, that she was your everyday princess, living in a privileged bubble filled with parties and balls and designer everything, and most of all, without an ounce of street smarts. Exactly why he'd delegated to his trusted operatives the task of finding her and delivering her home, until all attempts to find her had failed and it was clear he'd have to chase her down himself. Nobody had entertained any idea the Princess had the slightest clue about staying out of sight and eluding those searching for her for so long.

If he had to admit it, he held a grudging admiration for the way she'd done it, never staying in one place long enough to be noticed, jumping sideways and backward in her travels and always one infuriating step ahead, this latest move the most audacious, the most surprising.

But at the same time, she'd outsmarted herself, and the time for admiration, along with the hunt, was over. He had his prey all but in his sights. An island that hosted no more than four hundred guests at one time along with a handful of locals and casual workers.

And as the plane came in to land, the blood in his veins pumped fast and furious.

He had her.

CHAPTER ONE

ISABELLA CYCLED ALONG the palm-lined road leading from the café where she'd just finished her third lunch shift waiting tables, unable to stop a grin from splitting her face. Her third shift in a row, and now she'd been asked to do both lunch and dinner tomorrow!

She couldn't believe it. She, Princess Isabella d'Montcroix, actually had a job and was working. *Really* working at a *real* job, just like a normal person, and she hadn't messed up. Sure, they didn't know she was a princess, and in truth, she'd had to work at it. Memorising table numbers and orders and working out how to stack a table full of plates on one arm and not drop them on the way back to the kitchen while she was being yelled at by Chef to hurry up had almost done her head in—but she'd survived, and now she was being rewarded with more shifts.

Dappled sunlight played through the shadows, brief flashes of light amongst the twilight of the lush rainforest surrounds allowing glimpses of the cerulean lagoon to one side. It had rained this morning, a light shower that coupled with the day's sunshine, had heightened the earthy rainforest scent. Izzy breathed deeply of the heady combination of forest floor with the lagoon's salt air, a smell she would forever associate with the smell of freedom, and she grinned some more. Finally, she could feel the tension of the last few weeks slip away.

Finally, she was starting to believe that she was safe and could stop looking over her shoulder every other minute.

Hopefully for long enough to enjoy it.

But more than that, hopefully long enough to convince her brother to abandon his abhorrent plan to marry her off to one of his cronies.

Because there was no way she was going home until he did.

A van trundled past at the requisite twenty-five-kilometres-per-hour island speed limit, the driver lifting a hand to her as he passed. Jack, she realised, the owner of the café, on his way to meet the afternoon plane to pick up fresh fruit and vegetable supplies. She waved back, her heart skipping a beat as the bike wobbled, before she replaced her hand on the handlebars, steadying both her heart rate and the bike. Riding a bike had been another challenge, but here on the island, it was either that or walk, and she was rapidly conquering this new learned skill too, discovering muscles she'd never realised she had as she turned her bicycle up the road heading up the hill and away from the lagoon, towards the row of cabins let out to the casual workers who serviced the island's resort and hostel labour needs. Backpackers like they assumed she was, just another tourist from Europe working a few weeks or months to replenish travel funds before once more, moving on.

She jumped off when she met the steep path leading to her cabin, pushing her bike past pink and red flowering hibiscus bushes and waving to her neighbours, Sven and Inga relaxing on their small balcony. That was another thing she loved about the island. Everybody waved and said hello, whether you were a casual worker, a tourist or one of the sprinkling of island residents who'd lived on the island for generations.

'Come and join us,' said Inga, holding up her bottle of lager. 'We're celebrating surviving the climb up Mt Gower.'

'You did it?' Izzy asked, parking her bike against her veranda railing and unclipping her helmet. She had hair to colour tonight, part of the disguise she'd assumed to camouflage her blonde hair, but that could wait a little longer. Right now she wanted to hear about her neighbours' climb. The island boasted dozens of bush walks through its kentia palm and banyan tree subtropical rainforest coverage, with the eight-plus-hour return hike up the nearly kilometre-high mountain the number one challenge.

'Congratulations,' she said, pulling up a chair beside them as Inga pulled a beer from a six-pack and handed it to her.

Izzy smiled as she clinked longnecks with her neighbours before taking a sip of the amber liquid straight from the bottle. Another new skill she'd acquired since being in Australia. Her brother would be horrified if he could see her right now, and that made her smile widen. 'So tell me, what was it like?'

'Amazing,' Inge said. 'You have to do it. The views are breathtaking.'

Sven nodded after taking a long swallow. 'It's tough,

but worth it. You should definitely do it while you're here.'

'I will,' she said, excited at the prospect and loving the buzz of being able to decide what she wanted to do and then simply go do it without an entire palace deciding on whether or not it was an appropriate occupation for a princess before then planning it down to the tiniest detail, right down to laying out the appropriate outfit she should wear. It was liberating, this new freedom. Intoxicating. Addictive. 'I am definitely going to do that,' she said, making a promise to herself and sealing the deal with another sip of her beer. 'Cheers.'

Later that evening Isabella applied a fresh layer of chalk to her hair. She'd read that the best way to disguise yourself was not necessarily to add glasses or another disguise, but to take something away. She was taking away the platinum blonde, which was far too Princess Isabella for her liking. And now that every second woman seemed to have brightly coloured hair, nobody looked twice at hers. Job done, she checked out her hair in the mirror, now red and purple with the odd strip of teal. She smiled. Perfect. Nobody would guess she was a princess.

She made herself a mug of tea and stepped out onto her little porch in time to catch the dying rays of the sunset over the tops of the palm trees, painting the sky a brilliant red. She put her mug down and watched a while, in awe as the colours intensified, then shifted and softened. God, it was a gorgeous place to live.

She'd come here seeking sanctuary. A hideaway. But the longer she was here, the more she loved this island. Here, she was accepted for herself, not for her association with the royal Montcroix family of Rubanestein. And as much as she loved her European homeland and knew how privileged she was, it was refreshing to be somewhere where she could be known for herself, not just for being a princess.

Lord Howe Island was the perfect place to hide.

Here on this island, nobody grilled her about her accent because it seemed like every second person she'd met was from somewhere else.

Even better, not one person questioned why she was here, because everybody knew the answer. Because who wouldn't want to be here, on this island paradise?

Izzy smiled to herself as she headed inside to make a fresh mug of tea. Nobody in a million years would pick she was a European princess, and nobody could know, given her passport was safely tucked away in a safety deposit box in Sydney.

Nobody would find her here.

CHAPTER TWO

THE RUNWAY WAS little more than a short strip of tarmac between the neighbouring hills, the terminal no more than a shed, cows grazing on a nearby field. Theo took a moment at the top of the small flight of stairs to take it all in. The small-town vibe was a world away from the sumptuous palace overlooking the Mediterranean coastline that was Princess Isabella's home in the smallest principality in Europe, but maybe that was all part of her twisted logic to come here—because who would think to look for a precious princess in a place where luxury appeared to take a back seat?

But twisted logic it was, because now she was trapped, caught in the web of her own making.

He dragged in a breath as he set off down the stairs. The salty air was flavoured with avgas, but all Theo could smell was success.

Hell, forget smelling it, he was so close, he could taste it.

A group of travellers stood at the gate, waiting for the return flight to Sydney. A few families with children, a group of older people in leisure wear and a sprinkling of couples kitted out in hiking gear.

He scanned their faces. He hadn't come this far to lose

her now. But no, there were no princesses that he could see amongst their number.

'You must be Theo?' a broad Australian voice said, a sixty-something man with a weather-beaten face approaching, a sign bearing the name of Theo's accommodation in one hand. 'Tom Parker's my name,' he said, glancing at the leather duffel bag in Theo's hand. 'Any more luggage to collect?'

Theo shook his head; he wasn't planning on staying long. He didn't need it. 'No luggage,' he said.

'Right-o,' said Tom, 'let's get going.' And he led Theo through the tiny terminal to a late-model sedan in the car park just beyond.

'You here on holidays, Mr Mylonakos?' he said, eying Theo's suit and tie as he stashed Theo's carry-on in the boot. 'Lord Howe Island is the perfect spot to wind down.'

'A short one,' Theo said, opening the passenger door and sliding in. 'I'm meeting a friend.'

'Oh. Someone staying with us?' The car engine purred into life.

'I'm not sure.'

The man looked at him sideways.

'It's a surprise,' Theo said. Because it would be, and then he added a little white lie. 'It's her birthday.'

'Ah,' the older man said, smiling now, a twinkle lighting his eyes. 'Well, it shouldn't take long to find her on this island. Only so many places a person can hide.'

Theo allowed himself his first smile of the day. *Exactly what he'd been thinking.*

'What's her name then?'

'Erin,' Theo said, giving the name on the passport

she'd swapped with a girl she'd met in Sydney—the name she'd used on the travel documents to Lord Howe Island to try to elude anyone trying to find her. 'Erin Kowalski.'

The older man's brow puckered as he slid in behind the steering wheel. 'Nope, doesn't ring any bells.'

It was a long shot, he knew, but Theo handed him a photograph, of the Princess in a day dress, minus tiara, at a horse race. It was the most casual likeness he had of her, the wind had ruffled the ends of her blonde hair and the photographer had caught the excitement in her eyes as the horses had neared the finish line. It was the least regal photo he'd been able to find, because if the Princess was altering her appearance to fly under the radar, she wouldn't be wearing gowns and jewels now.

'Hmm,' the man said, his brow knotted as he stroked his chin.

Theo's pulse lurched. 'You've seen her?'

'Not so sure about that,' he said, as he handed the photo back. 'She looks a bit like a waitress I saw working in the café, except her hair's a different colour, and I'm pretty sure her name wasn't Erin.' He shrugged, handing the photo back. 'Then again, all these young people look alike these days, don't they?'

Theo thanked him as he took it back, not entirely defeated. He'd check out the café, of course, but he hadn't expected finding her would be that easy, even on an island the size of a postage stamp. Besides, the Princess was hardly waitress material. She'd been surrounded by staff eager to do her every bidding ever since the day she was born. She'd never worked a real job a day in her life. No, more likely he'd find her lounging on a beach making herself comfortable somewhere.

'I hope you don't mind,' Tom said, 'but I thought I'd give you a brief tour of the island before I drop you at the lodge. Help you get your bearings.'

Theo suppressed his irritation. Now that he was here, all Theo wanted to do was to get to work as soon as possible. He wasn't a tourist. He didn't need a tour. He just needed to find the Princess—before someone else did.

The car set off slowly—painfully slowly it seemed, but apparently that was the speed limit here—along the road bordering the runway that bisected the island, the driver still talking, pointing out the bowling club, the hospital, the dive school, while Theo only half listened, more interested in searching the faces of the cyclists they passed going the other way, looking for a familiar feature. Until he heard something that made him prick up his ears and swivel his head.

'Wait, wait. What did you say?' he asked.

'About the waitress the other night, you mean?'

Theo nodded.

'Well, she was getting a right dressing-down from the chef about being too slow and having to lift her game, poor girl. I thought she was about to burst into tears at one stage.'

Theo's ears pricked up. He spun his head back, more interested now. 'What girl?'

'The girl in the café. The one I mentioned before.'

Theo didn't expect to find his runaway princess employed and working. But if she was—and turned out to be a no-good waitress—what were the chances?

'But her name wasn't Erin, this girl in the café?'

'No, that doesn't ring a bell at all, but I can't help thinking she looked a bit like that girl in the picture you showed me.' He shrugged as they turned right up a hill, buildings set either side, a general store and some kind of town hall. 'Then again, it's a few days back now.' He nodded to the side as they passed a café. 'That's where I saw her, whoever she was. But I'd remember it if her name was Erin. Struck me at the time that it rhymed with something, except I can't remember what it was now.' He chortled. 'Not to worry, it'll come to me, sure as eggs.'

The hairs on the back of Theo's neck prickled and he had to resist the urge to yell at Tom to stop so he could jump from the car and check for himself. Could it be her? But what would a spoiled princess know about waitressing? Up until now, she hadn't stayed in one spot long enough to find work.

But he said nothing. There was no need to alarm Tom that there was more to his story than what he'd made out, especially if there was no guarantee it was her. Equally, there was no need to rush. If it was her, and the Princess was so confident that her little scheme to slip her pursuers had succeeded and that she could afford to stop a while and put down some roots, then she wasn't going anywhere in a hurry.

Meanwhile he'd book for dinner tonight at the café and check it out for himself.

They left the café behind, the road rising towards a turn-off that signalled Ned's Beach, where Tom mentioned that he could feed the fish for a nominal sum. 'Got any idea what activities you'd like to try your hand at while you're here?' Tom asked. 'We've got diving or snorkelling on the coral reef, or there's game fishing out near Ball's Pyramid. Lizzie, our manager, can book you into anything you feel like.'

'I'll think about it,' Theo lied, knowing there'd be no time to play the tourist. His job was to find the Princess and get her home.

'Of course, that's it!' said Tom slapping his knee beside him. 'I don't know why it's taken so long to remember; it rhymes with Lizzie of course.'

'What does?'

'The name of the girl in the café. I knew it would come to me. The chef called her Izzy.'

Izzy?

Isabella.

And Theo wanted to punch his fist in the air with victory.

He had her.

CHAPTER THREE

THE RESTAURANT WAS buzzing when Izzy turned up for the dinner shift.

'Thank god you're here,' one of her colleagues said as she rushed past with her arms full of dirty dishes. 'It's going to be mental.'

'What's going on?' Izzy asked.

'Palmtrees has lost its generator,' the head waiter said, referring to one of the island's fully catered lodges, 'and their fridges are out. They're sending all their guests here.'

Izzy aproned up and started work. She'd been on the island long enough to work out that with their fridges out, it meant an extra hundred or so hungry people out looking for a meal. No wonder it was so busy.

For two hours she worked solidly, darting between tables, the kitchen and the bar, taking orders and fetching meals and drinks. She'd barely clear a table and it would be full again, and the whole process would start over. She was never more grateful for her earlier shifts.

'Can you get table thirty?' the manager called, backing through the kitchen door, her arms full of plates.

'On my way,' she said, picking up a couple of menus and threading her way through the bustling restaurant.

She knew where table thirty was. A table for two, tucked right up the back. She smiled as she approached. A dark-haired man, sitting alone.

He looked up, as she neared, his dark eyes scowling, his gaze as combative as the hard lines of his jaw. Unnerving. Clearly not impressed at having to wait for service, but who could blame him? 'I'm so sorry to keep you waiting,' she started, wanting to head off any cause for aggravation. 'We're very busy tonight.' She placed a menu in front of him, and then one at the empty chair opposite.

'I'm eating alone,' he said, his words terse, and Izzy pulled the menu back and hugged it against her chest. Why she felt like she needed protection, she wasn't sure, but there was something in the deep timbre of his voice that sounded like it was being kept on a tight leash. Had he been stood up or had he argued with his partner and decided to eat alone? Was that the reason for his anger? Although he didn't look like any tourist, more like one of the consultants from the mainland who visited the island for a day or two to call upon their clients.

'A drink then, on the house,' she said, attempting another smile, hoping to appease, 'for keeping you waiting so long.'

A muscle twitched in his jaw, but it was his eyes that unnerved her. The way he looked at her, almost like he was looking inside her. And then he leaned sideways in his chair, crossed his long legs and smiled, and Izzy was taken aback by the transformation. It could just have been the play of light as he moved, the light and shadow moving, but it appeared that his jawline had relaxed, the hard line of his mouth softening, his lips suddenly sensual, and dark-lashed eyes creasing at the corners. All of it framed with thick dark hair. A disarmingly good-looking man when he smiled, and Izzy's heart lurched and found herself thinking, what a waste he was alone.

'Tell me,' he said, giving the menu a cursory glance before looking back at her. 'What would you recommend?'

She blinked, feeling off balance with the change in his mood. She reeled off the list of specials, the kingfish, the fillet steak and the lobster medallions, trying and failing not to notice how well his fine knit sweater skimmed his broad chest when he sat back like that.

'What would you order?' he asked, when she had finished.

'The kingfish is very popular. It's a local speciality. But my personal favourite would be the paella.'

He cocked an eyebrow, sitting forward now, like he was genuinely interested. 'Why so?'

She smiled, her mind going back to the tiny fishing villages that dotted the short Mediterranean coastline of Rubanestein, and of the street cafés far below the palace with their braziers alight, topped with vast pans filled with seafood and rice, the warm night air filled with the scent of salt and saffron, the sizzle and smoke of the burners, and the warm-hearted conviviality of the people. 'It reminds me of my home,' she said, feeling an unexpected pang of something approximating homesickness. Not that she had been free to roam the streets of the villages or enjoy the bonhomie of the villagers by herself, always accompanied by her body-guards and minders. Always. Never free. Not like here.

And the homesickness was suddenly snuffed out on a familiar tide of resentment.

'Where is home?'

His words interrupted her thoughts. She'd been miles away. Continents. An entire hemisphere. She shook her head to clear it. 'A little place in Europe,' she said, screwing up her nose. 'You wouldn't have heard of it. Would you like to order now?'

'I'll have the paella,' he said, taking her recommendation, ordering a glass of Tasmanian pinot noir to go with it. He handed her back the menu. 'Thank you for helping me decide,' he said, turning up the warmth in his smile so that it zinged all the way to her toes.

Not just good-looking, she told herself as she weaved her way back through the bustling tables to the kitchen. Seriously good-looking. Even drop-dead gorgeous when he smiled like that.

She returned from the bar with the bottle, pouring the ruby-coloured liquid into his glass, so conscious he was watching her that her skin tingled and her cheeks burned, and it was all she could do to stop the hand holding the bottle from shaking.

'Will that be all?' she asked, her task completed, relieved she hadn't spilled a drop given the intensity of his scrutiny.

'For now,' he said, and there was that zing again.

Millie winked when they crossed paths in the kitchen. 'You took your time out there,' she said, nodding in the direction of table thirty. 'Who's the hunk? Someone you know?'

'No. He just wanted my advice on what to order.'

'Then I think he fancies you,' she said. 'He can't take his eyes off you.'

'Rubbish,' she said, but Millie was already away with her next order, and Izzy similarly loaded her arms up with her next delivery, discounting Millie's comment. But as she worked the tables, she wasn't so sure. Every time she happened to glance over in that direction, her eyes were snagged by his and he would smile, sending warmth rippling down her spine that persisted, even when she'd turned away. She didn't have to look up to know he was still watching her. She could feel his eyes in the tingling of her skin and the fizz of her blood. And she sensed with a woman's intuition that he wasn't just staring at her because he was impatient for his meal to be served.

For a woman who'd never before experienced this zing of attraction, an attraction not based on her title and how that might work for him, but an attraction between a man and a woman, it was as unexpected as it was intoxicating.

'Enjoy your meal,' Izzy said, placing a plate in front of him and the steaming pan in the centre of the table. And yet instead of the fragrant spiced paella, all she seemed to be able to smell was this man, and the warm, clean scent of him. It was unnerving being so aware of a man. Not only because it was an unfamiliar experience, but because it seemed too personal. Too intimate. She backed away as soon as the pan was down, aiming to get away and back to the kitchen as quickly as possible, but not before he could ask, 'What's your name?'

She paused in her retreat, laced the fingers of her hands together in front of her. 'Izzy.'

He leant his head to one side, dark eyes silently appraising. 'You remind me of someone.'

Her stomach lurched, even as she told herself there was no reason to worry. There was no reason to think this man knew who she was. It was the fear she'd been living with for these last six weeks rearing its ugly head once again. The constant fear of being discovered. She pushed loose tendrils of her hair behind her ears, forced a smile to her lips, aiming for casual interest, when she felt a bundle of nerves. 'Do I?'

He shook his head, as if shaking the idea away. 'But no. Her name was something quite different.'

Relief. She smiled and felt herself relax. 'I'm sure we all have a double or two out there somewhere in the world.'

'Yes,' he said, his eyes back on hers, smile back in place. 'That must be it. Very nice to meet you though, Izzy from a little place in Europe I wouldn't have heard of.'

Izzy headed to another table to clear their plates, feeling a little sideswiped by the encounter. Something didn't sit quite right. Something that had turned an exciting stomach-fluttering encounter into something entirely more unnerving. Because the smile that had accompanied his words was empty—words that had included both her name and her home continent, when he'd offered nothing. And even if not specific—if he'd been looking for Princess Isabella it might be enough...

She dropped off the dirty dishes in the kitchen and stole a glance between the bar and the glassware that hung suspended upside down from the rails above it.

He was eating his meal, she noticed, but not like a diner thoroughly taken with the experience, content to

concentrate on the food on his plate, or scrolling through
his phone as if searching for a whisper of internet, but
as if going through the motions when he had another,
far more important duty to perform. Like scanning the
restaurant and taking notice of every movement. As if
searching. Always searching. He turned his head towards
the bar and she ducked behind it. Before he saw her?
Who could tell? All she knew was that this unsettled
feeling in her stomach wasn't going to go away until
she could get away.

And she hadn't got this far without taking heed of
her gut feelings.

If he didn't know who she was, then her absence
wouldn't matter. And if he did—at least it might afford
her a head start.

Millie obviously took her interest in her table-for-one
for something other than what it was. 'How are you getting on with Mr Dreamboat? Has he asked you about
dessert yet?' She followed it with a wicked wink that
suggested she hadn't been talking about any sweet on
the menu.

Izzy scanned the restaurant. The tables were empty-
ing, the rush over. 'Do you think it would be all right, if
I finished my shift now?'

Millie's eyes narrowed suspiciously, her lips curled.
'Are you sure you're not just wanting to sneak off early
with Mr Table Number Thirty?'

'No! It's just—' She scrambled for an excuse. 'I'm
feeling a little weird.'

'Hey, it's okay, I was kidding. And you do look a bit
peaky. Go on, you've already worked longer than ros-
tered.' She leaned closer to whisper in her ear. 'And don't

tell anyone I told you this, but Chef is really happy with how quickly you've picked the job up. Any chance you could come back and do another evening shift tomorrow?'

The praise should have bolstered her spirits more than it did. Instead, it was only relief she felt. 'I'll be here,' Izzy promised, crossing fingers behind her back. Because with luck, she would, and this man would be nowhere to be seen. She swiped off her apron and collected her bag, slipping out the back door with a wave and a quiet goodbye to the kitchen staff.

She was probably overreacting, dashing away like this. No doubt she'd feel foolish about it later, but it was better to be cautious. Better to be sure. The interaction with the stranger today had felt both exciting and unsettling. Already she felt relieved to be away from his presence, and out in the clear island air where she could think straight. Her bike was propped up against the building where she'd left it. The wind was gusting, whipping at her hair even as she struggled to pull on her helmet. She'd heard mention of a storm cell possibly tracking close to the island. That might make things interesting for the next few days.

She cycled off, proud of herself for cornering around the side without having to put her feet down. Then she was at the road and the restaurant was behind her, and with every pedal of her feet, she felt the tension leach out of her. The wind rattled through the palm trees lining either side of the road, the fronds dancing on the wind, almost as if chattering to each other, while the ocean waves boomed as they crashed into the lagoon's coral reef. She breathed deeply of the fertile air, laced with salt.

She loved this island. It was friendly and so easy to live in and, best of all, she was free, with nobody to tell her what she could and couldn't do and—she shuddered—who she would marry.

Two cyclists going the other way waved to her, a van ambled slowly past delivering a load of diners back to their accommodation, but other than that, the road was empty and dark. Anywhere else in the world, that might feel threatening, or even feel scary. But here she felt safe.

Already, her sudden departure seemed ridiculous. She'd imagined the threat. Blown it up in her mind like the wind gusting off the sea. Soon she'd be back in her cabin and a mysterious dark-eyed man and his unsettling gaze would be nothing more than a distant memory.

The headlights of a car appeared behind, slowly catching up to her, and giving her a wide berth as it passed. She waved but it was too dark to see if anyone waved back—but no matter, as this was her turn. Just up the hill a bit was the driveway to her simple cabin.

She turned into her driveway as another car cruised by—or was it the same one doubling back? There weren't that many cars on the island. She stepped behind a hibiscus tree and waited until it disappeared over the hill. Okay, so she was officially paranoid. They'd probably just missed their turn-off.

With relief she let herself into her accommodation and snapped on the kettle. She really needed a calming cup of chamomile tea. Ten minutes later, she was sitting on her sofa, Andrea Bocelli playing on her speakers, with shoes off and aching feet up and a mug of tea in hands, feeling that all was once again right in Izzy's world.

The knock on the door changed that, a knock on the

door that came with no accompanying call from Inga or Sven or anyone who would know to do that. She jumped to her feet, for the first time having cause to question the island's lack of door locks; something that had seemed quaint and old world-y when she'd first been told, something that now felt a whole lot more threatening. All was silent outside, but she could feel a dark presence, malevolent and waiting.

'Who is it?' she called, even though she knew by the chill in her spine and the smothering weight of silence that answered her call. Isabella looked around, needing to think fast. Whoever it was could turn the handle and walk right in. But there was a window in the bedroom behind her. She had no idea where she was going to run—there was no time to formulate a plan. All she knew was that she had to get away. 'Hold on,' she said, infusing a degree of brightness into her voice that she didn't feel, already halfway there. 'I'll be right there.'

She had the window up and the screen off with one leg over the sill and the other close behind, momentum propelling her forward, when she heard a deep voice say, 'Going somewhere, Princess?'

CHAPTER FOUR

IT WAS DARK behind the cabin, all shifting shadows and slapping leaves, but she knew instantly from his voice that it was him—*the man from table thirty*—and she knew she'd been right and that she had to get away. But she had too much momentum to back up. She tumbled headfirst out the window and collided with a wall that shouldn't be there, a wall that encircled her with bands of steel, arresting her fall. 'Oof,' she said, as the air was forced from her lungs. Flight no longer an option, her fight reflex kicked in. 'Let me go!' she said, her heart beating frantically in her chest, her legs kicking, her hands beating at her captor's chest.

'I have to hand it to you, Princess,' he said, totally unmoved by her efforts to free herself. 'You've been very clever. But your little game is over, and now it's time to take you home.'

'You're mad,' she said, still writhing against the wall of his body. The all too hot and hard wall of his body. 'I don't know what you're talking about.'

'So why all that effort to sneak out the window?'

'Because you're stalking me! And now you're making up some crazy story to justify kidnapping me.' She squirmed and tugged, harder this time, but still to no effect, except for the damning friction she created in her efforts. 'Let me go!'

'You must have known that someone would catch up with you eventually. You're lucky that it's me. And now, to quote the classic line from the movies, it would be easier for us both if you came quietly.'

Quietly?

Now there was an idea. There was nothing on this island to confirm her true identity—all her ID was in Erin's name. It was her word against his and who was going to believe a man who wanted to take her from the island against her will? She opened her mouth, only to feel his hand clamp hard over her open mouth, smothering her attempt to scream.

'There's no point fighting the inevitable, Princess. Prince Rafael wants you home safe and sound, and that's where I'm taking you.'

Izzy had always known what being caught meant—an end to her new-found freedom and the beginning of a new hell, a forced marriage to a man she could never love. But it was hearing mention of her hateful brother's name that tipped her over the edge. She writhed and bucked, kicking out at him, trying to find traction even as he held her high and hard against him. But her feet couldn't reach the ground and all she succeeded in doing was landing kicks at his legs. Not that he so much as flinched. Her brother had sent a robot to hunt her down, the man must be made of metal or stone. But curse Rafael and his man-mountain, she wasn't going back. Not if it meant she would serve as a pawn in one of Rafael's selfish schemes.

'Ngh, ngh!' she muttered against his hand, finally

finding a crack between his fingers to spit out the words, 'I'll see my brother rot in hell first!'

And the hands wrapped around her eased a fraction, as a deep voice whispered in her ear. 'Thank you, Princess. You can stop with the pretence now.'

And Isabella knew she'd been had. She went limp in his arms, the fight gone out of her.

'That's more like it,' he said, and swung her into his arms.

'What are you doing?' she protested, as her body slammed against his chest.

'Taking you back through the front door so you can pack your things. Although, if you prefer, I can toss you back through the window the same way you came out?'

He was laughing at her now. And yes, so maybe it wouldn't be the most elegant way to enter the cabin, but she might actually prefer it if he did. It was impossible to think with his arms under her back and legs, impossible to think when she was this close and when his every movement generated friction where their bodies rubbed. And she so needed space to think. Whatever this man thought, she wasn't about to give up her freedom, just because he'd found her. She'd find a way to get away. She couldn't go back. Not to what her brother had planned for her.

'Who are you?' she demanded, turning on her most imperious voice, a voice that had been known to turn grown courtiers into simpering wrecks. 'Why are you manhandling me like this?'

He laughed out loud this time, a gruff laugh that only served to ratchet up her ill humour, as he bounded up the steps to the veranda like she weighed nothing, her body jolting against his firm torso—his *too hard, too hot* torso—with every stride. And the more she tried to squirm away, the more friction she caused. Curse the man, why couldn't he have felt cold, like the stone he looked like he'd been carved from?

'You have the nerve to laugh at me?' she said, if only to pretend she thought nothing of the sizzling heat where their bodies met.

'I don't know who you think you're ordering around, Princess,' he said, 'but it's wasted on me. I'm Theo Mylonakos. The Prince wants you home where you'll be safe, and it's my job to get you there.'

'The Prince wants? *The Prince wants?* And you pander to him like he's the only person who matters. What about what *I* want? Why does what I want count for nothing?'

'You are a princess of Rubanestein,' he said, using his foot to kick the front door closed behind them. 'Your duty lies with your country and its people.'

His words rankled. She didn't have to be lectured about her duty, she'd lived for nothing more than her country and its people for most of her twenty-five years, all through the reign of her father and his premature death, the coronation of her brother and the honeymoon period of his reign—in fact, right up until the time her brother had announced that her premier duty to the principality was to be sold off like she was no more than his personal chattel in order to cover his gambling losses.

'And if I refuse to go?'

He let her go so unexpectedly that her knees buckled beneath her. She would have collapsed to the floor but for the large hands that seized her waist, arresting her fall. Air whooshed from her lungs, not only out of shock, but because there was that burn again, this time at her waist. He had big hands. Long-fingered hands that made such a mockery of the fabric of her T-shirt that it might just as well have been made of silk—gossamer-thin silk that transmitted the heat of his hands to her senses. She could feel the heat from every pad of his fingers, she could feel the press of every single digit of his hand against her flesh.

It was sheer hell. Yet at the same time, it was mesmerising. *Hypnotising.* She knew she should protest at his intrusion, at the personal invasion of her space and her body, but with the sensation spiralling through her flesh, sending sparks to places she'd never felt the touch of sparks—in the tightness of her nipples, in the aching flesh between her thighs, sensation stalled any immediate protest.

She felt his breath fan across her face, and she looked up to see him looking down at her, his face inches away, his eyes dark, his expression stern, like she was some kind of problem to him. And only then did she realise that she must have thrown out her arms in desperation and that her own hands were full, clinging to his firm shoulders.

She tested her knees and found her footing. He was too close, his masculine scent invading her space, and she needed to get away.

But it was he who let go before she did.

She wobbled just a little as she spun away, feeling relief that his hands were gone, at the same time feeling their absence—feeling the lack of his proximity—like a loss. *Madness.* But the heat hadn't gone. It had moved, surging into her cheeks at her own ridiculous thoughts.

She turned back, hoping that he took her reddened cheeks as embarrassment, or better still, outrage. Outrage.

Now there was the preferable option. And she should feel outraged. She jerked up her chin and puffed out her chest. 'I could order you fed to the palace eels for man-handling me the way you just did.'

'The way I saved you, you mean?'

She snorted. 'Some saviour. Bundling me up like a trussed-up turkey. Dropping me like a stone.'

'I did prevent you from falling to the floor.'

'And I should thank you for that?'

'I don't expect thanks. I'll settle for you packing your things and coming with me.'

'Then you're in for a disappointment. I'm not leaving.'

He took a step closer. 'Sorry to disappoint you, Princess,' he snarled, 'but you don't have a choice.'

His eyes had turned obsidian, the angles of his face turned harsher and more defined, his lips a terse line, and Izzy wondered if she'd imagined the softening in his features she'd thought she'd witnessed at the restaurant. Maybe it had been a trick of the light, because there was not one iota of softness in his features now. His eyes were like stone. His jawline constructed of rigid angles. Hard, unforgiving and immovable. Like the man himself.

He spun on his heel and headed into the bedroom she'd so recently tried to escape from and slammed the window shut. Then he pulled her backpack from the top of the wardrobe and threw it on the bed before stepping back to make way for her. He crossed his arms. 'Now, pack your things. You're staying with me tonight, where I can keep an eye on you. We leave on the first flight.'

'No! I told you, I am not leaving. Even if I agreed to go with you, which I am not, there's no way I could leave tomorrow anyway.'

'Give it up, Princess,' he growled, 'this is getting old already. You've had your fun. Playtime is over, and now it's time to go home.'

She stamped her foot. 'This is not playtime. Don't treat me like a child.'

'Then don't act like one.'

The man was beyond infuriating. 'Look,' she said, pinching her nose and breathing deep, taking a moment to calm herself down. This man was clearly easy to aggravate, so maybe it was time to be a bit more placatory. Hopefully a bit more persuasive. 'So, you've found me— congratulations—you win. But does it matter if it's a day or two later that I arrive home? Because I can't leave tomorrow. I'm working a shift tomorrow evening.'

He shook his head as if dealing with a recalcitrant child, as clearly, he regarded her. 'Forget it. You don't need to work.'

'That's hardly the point. The point is, I have a job and I promised to work tomorrow evening's shift.'

He scoffed. 'You're a waitress. I'm sure they'll manage to cover you.'

It wasn't just the words. It was the disdain that put her back up, his thorough disregard for her work—for *the* work—as if waiting tables was so lowly that it was no kind of job at all. And suddenly she was over with all attempts at peacemaking. She was livid. 'How dare you? How dare you talk about duty and what my duty is when

you have no idea what duty entails? I made a commit-
ment to this business, and I intend to see it through. So,
if you insist on taking me back to Rubanestein, against
my will I might add, then you're going to have to wait
until *I'm* ready to go.'

His lip curled. 'Nice speech. So, when are you going
to start packing, Princess, or do you expect me to do it
for you?'

'So, wait a day! Twenty-four hours. Where's the harm
in that?'

'Haven't you heard? There's a cyclone hovering off
the coast. I'm not prepared for it to get any closer and
risk our chances of getting off this island.'

'Of course I've heard. Everyone's heard. But we're
not in the path. It's hardly a problem.'

He said nothing. Just cast his eyes in the direction of
her backpack. The man was insufferable.

'In that case,' she said, crossing her arms over her chest,
'you do it.' She was hardly going to help him. She had
more important things to do, like work out how she was
going to get away. Her teeth played with her lip. She could
escape while he was in the other room, of course, the door
didn't have a lock, and she'd have a lead of a second or
two before he realised. But this man was fit. And he was
built. Slamming into his chest had told her that, and that
lead of a second or two would evaporate into nothingness
the moment he caught on. She needed a better plan. And
she had at the very most one night to come up with one.

He looked back at her, his eyebrows raised, his lips
curled into a sardonic smile. But he said nothing, simply
opened the small wardrobe and peeled from the hang-
ers the few shirts and a sundress she had inside. Turned

to a small chest of drawers and pulled open a drawer and scooped out a handful of lace bras and panties and smalls, before he seemed to realise what he was holding and rapidly looked away as he shoved them into the backpack.

The next drawer's contents of jeans and shorts followed her underwear into the pack. 'Is that it?' he said, sounding like he must have missed something.

'Of course not, you'll find the ball gowns and tiaras in the gilded chest under the bed.'

He made a move to glance below the bed before thinking better of it and giving her a glare that could have stripped paint. 'Funny,' he said.

'I thought so,' she said, feeling her lips tweak in spite of the desperate circumstances. 'It sure gave me a smile.'

He growled, a low, deep growl that spoke of his frustration with her. Of his frustration to be done with her. Of his desperation to be rid of her.

'Tomorrow,' he said. 'We fly out tomorrow.'

'No!'

He shook his head. 'You don't have a say in this.'

'Wow. You sound just like my brother. He doesn't think I should have a say in anything either.'

He grunted. 'Maybe he has a point.'

'Or maybe he's just a controlling bastard like you. Congratulations on finding your soulmate. I hope you're both very happy together.'

His eyes turned to slate. His nostrils flared. 'Are you done?'

'Oh, but you provide such rich material. I'm sure I'll find more.'

'Excellent. Then while you're finding things, maybe

you can gather up your toiletries in the bathroom and we can get out of here.'

'Why do I need to go anywhere? You know where I'm going to be tomorrow evening—working my shift at the restaurant, no doubt to be glowered at every minute of my shift by your own uncharming visage.'

'Nice try, Princess. Leave you here tonight and discover tomorrow that you've done a runner? It's not going to happen. Now go and get the rest of your things.'

'Where do you think I'm going to run? There's something like two flights out a day and I won't be catching either of them, because, like I told you, I am committed to a shift tomorrow night.'

'So you say. But I can't take that risk. You're coming with me tonight and we're flying out tomorrow. Together.'

Her arms flew wide before slapping back against her thighs. 'What is your problem? I've already been gone for weeks. What difference is twenty-four hours going to make?'

He zipped up the backpack. 'Don't you realise what you're risking, Princess? You leave yourself open to any kind of attack. And in doing so, you expose Rubanestein in the process.'

'And what, pray tell, do you think might happen to me? Do you think there's a chance that I might be kidnapped and taken somewhere against my will?' She snorted. 'Imagine that!'

He growled. 'I'm not kidnapping you. I'm rescuing you from yourself and your foolish actions.'

She put her hands on her hips. 'I am twenty-five

years old, and you are insisting on taking me somewhere against my will. I'd call that kidnapping.'

'No, I'm safely returning you to the place where you belong, because if I worked out who you really are, don't you think that anyone else who is no doubt searching for you will?'

Her head snapped up at the thought that others might also be pursuing her. But no. He was trying to frighten her. Of course, he would try to scare her. 'You're bluffing.'

He said nothing. Just stared at her as he stood rock solid in front of her, and his silence slid uncomfortably down her spine, dislodging her rock-solid faith in her argument. 'So tell me, who else is supposedly looking for me?'

'Don't fool yourself into believing that I'm the only one. You've been missing in action so long that, no matter how much the palace has tried to dampen down speculation, your absence has been noted. The fact you missed the Prince's birthday ball three weeks ago only ramped up speculation that you'd run away and were on the loose.'

She made a move to interject and he cut her off with a slash of one hand.

'Don't you see? A runaway princess. Alone. Unprotected. Don't you realise the danger you've put yourself in, not to mention the embarrassment you're causing your country?'

His words stung Isabella's psyche. She hated the thought that her actions might result in embarrassment to Rubanestein, but she knew without a shadow of a doubt that if the true reason for her fleeing was made public, it would cause more damage to her country and the Prince than mere embarrassment. But there was no point trying to explain that to this man-mountain.

Izzy swallowed and spun away. Why did life have to be so complicated? All she'd wanted to do was escape from her brother and his demands and live life on her own terms. And not only was that not acceptable but now there were apparently rogue actors pursuing her?

She took a deep breath as she stared out into the dark. Tried to think. Tried to apply logic to the situation and not let his words frighten her. After all, this was a man who was trying to convince her to go with him and go quietly. Why wouldn't he try everything to make her accede to his every demand? She spun back around. 'But you have me now. You know where I am. I'm supposedly "safe" with you. So where's the risk with waiting one more day? Why should I feel frightened?'

'You should feel frightened, Princess, because, if anyone else catches up with you, I doubt you'll be bargaining for just one extra day.'

Her mouth went dry. If he was trying to frighten her, he was succeeding. 'What does that mean?'

'It means you're lucky I found you first. You're safe with me. I'll get you home.'

'Then maybe I should take my chances with whoever else is after me. Because I'm not safe with anyone who wants to return me to Rubanestein.'

'Stop being ridiculous. Think about your safety if you can't think about your country. I'm taking you back to your home where you'll be safe.'

'That's rubbish. You say I'm in danger here, but if you take me back, you'll be delivering me right back into the lion's den. Why do you think I ran? I'm not some rebellious teenager. Hasn't it occurred to you that I had my reasons for running?'

'I know, you did. You have a conflict with your brother.' He shrugged. 'It's understandable that you would be envious and it's equally understandable that you'd be angry and want to embarrass him.'

'Wait. What? Envious? What are you talking about?'

'Give it up, Princess. You're twelve months older than Rafael and yet, due to Rubanestein's traditional rules of succession, it is he who is on the throne and not you. It must have been a blow to see your younger brother accede to the throne when even the British monarchy, the oldest and most famous royal institution in the world, has modernised its rules so that the crown is passed down the line of succession not according to male-preference primogeniture.'

Izzy blinked, unable to believe what she was hearing. Unable to process it. She half-laughed, half-snorted, a very unladylike-*un-princess-like* snort. 'Is that what my dear brother told you? That I'm envious of him because he's on the throne and not me?'

'Why else would you come up with this little act of rebellion, if not to make some kind of statement?'

'Seriously, do I look like somebody who hungers to be on the throne? I've known my entire life that, failing a disaster, I would never accede to the throne. I have always been good with that. Do you really think I ran away because I'm in a snit?' She shook her head. 'You underestimate me, Mr Mylonakos, by a long way.'

He blinked. Slowly. 'Whatever, Prince Rafael is concerned for your safety and wants you escorted safely home.'

'That's a joke. He's never been concerned for anything other than his own well-being. He doesn't care for me. He doesn't care for anyone or anything other than how they can be of use to him.'

'Then why is he so keen to have you returned home, if he cares so little for you, his sister, his own flesh and blood?'

'Because he's racked up millions of Euros in debt and the Treasurer-General had the intestinal fortitude to prevent Rafael from getting his filthy hands in the Public Treasury.'

'What does that have to do with you?'

'Everything. He made a deal with one of his cronies.' She let that sink in for a moment waiting for him to join the dots. She saw the frown draw his brows together, creasing his brow. She witnessed the exact moment when realisation dawned on him, his dark eyes incredulous.

'Yes, Mr Mylonakos. He sold me. That's why he's so desperate to get me back in the palace under his control. So, he can carry out his plan to marry me off to the creep who's going to bail him out.'

His tense features relaxed. The corners of his mouth tweaked up. He shook his head. 'You've had weeks to come up with a story and that's the best you could manage? Don't you think that's just a bit melodramatic?'

'It's the truth!'

'So you say. But your response is straight out of the playbook. Prince Rafael said you'd say something like that.'

'Because it's the truth and he knows it!'

'Sure. Last I heard, Rubanestein was a modern European principality. What you are suggesting is positively medieval.'

She clenched her teeth. 'I see you've met my brother. He and his appalling wedding deal are the reasons I'm not going back.'

He shook his head. 'Princess—'

'Stop calling me princess. My name is Izzy.'

'I can't call you that. You're a princess. Princess Isabella.'

'Then why do you make it sound like an insult?'

Did he? If he did, it was because he was sick of the chase. He was sick of the arguments. Responsibility came with being an adult. He had no patience for people who shirked their responsibilities, preferring the easy life, ungrateful for the hand they'd been dealt.

He had people on his books who wanted to be rescued. Who desperately needed to be rescued. People who were a whole lot more deserving than this spoilt runaway who seemed intent on wasting his time.

Of course, he hadn't expected her to come without a fight, but she could have come up with something a bit more original than her evil brother who wanted to marry her off to settle the gambling debts story that she'd spun. Nothing in his research had so much as hinted at the Prince having a gambling problem.

'I won't call you Izzy. You are Princess Isabella d'Montcroix of Rubanestein. It's about time you started acting like it. Now, we're leaving. You can wash whatever that is out of your hair when you get to my apartment.'

'Won't I be in even more risk of being recognised if I

do wash out the colour? What if someone does recognise me and tries to snatch me away from you for ransom?'

He was beginning to think it was a good idea. 'Maybe I'll let them,' he said. 'It would save me a whole lot of grief.'

She laughed. She actually had the audacity to laugh.

'That wasn't a joke, Princess.'

'If I didn't know better,' she said, 'I'd be starting to think that I'm getting under your skin.'

'Don't flatter yourself, Princess.'

'Stop calling me Princess!'

He smiled around gritted teeth. 'Now who's getting under whose skin?'

CHAPTER FIVE

HER BACKPACK WAS zipped and stowed in his car and with nothing of hers left in her cabin, there was no choice for her but to begrudgingly settle into the passenger seat of his rental car. But she was far from settled. She was still thinking, still trying to buy time, still trying to work out a way to escape her captor, still rattled by the strange effect he had on her setting the nerves alight under her skin.

She shivered, wishing she could forget the impact this man had on her senses, and focus on her more immediate problem. This man had assured her that she was safe with him, but how could she believe him? There was no safety while his goal was to return her to the prison of the Rubanestein palace and to a soulless, loveless future.

She *had* to get away. She just had to work out how.

She thought about all she knew about him—about the mysterious dark-eyed man who'd all but bewitched her in the restaurant with his earnest gaze, and a smile that had transformed him into warmth. A warmth that had disappeared the moment he'd followed her to her cabin and hovered outside her door, a dark and malevolent presence. And that was before snatching her into his arms outside her window and turning her mind to the conflict between the outrage that he had dared to do that, and the unwanted distraction of the heat she felt where their bodies had connected.

That, and his story that he was somehow now her saviour. Surely saviours were supposed to be more recognisable. Like a hero who catches a runaway skier before they plunge headlong into a ravine, or the firefighter who runs into a burning building to save a baby lying in its cot, or the heroine who stops her car at the scene of a car crash to give a victim life-saving CPR.

Like an angel.

The concept of saviour hardly applied to a man who insisted on taking her back to her odious brother, and to the marriage and hellish life he intended to commit her to.

Similarly, the concept hardly applied to a man who might even be acting for someone other than her brother—one of those "rogue actors" he'd implied were also after her. But if he were a rogue actor, he was making a big mistake pretending to be her saviour by promising to take her home.

Big mistake.

The sky was dark, the moon and stars hidden behind the clouds, and it was only the car's headlights that cut a swath through the swaying palms either side to illuminate the road ahead. The slow way forward. The speed limit ensured the car could move at little more than a crawl. She could see from his set features in the glow of the dashboard lights that it was killing him to have to proceed so slowly.

She looked out her window. She could open her door, she mused, roll into the undergrowth on the side of the road, and run. At this speed it shouldn't kill her. And it would have to take him a moment to realise she'd made a dash for freedom, stop the car and come after her. It might not be enough time for her to find a place to hide, but with the rising wind he might not hear her running over the rattle of palm leaves.

Although where she might go then...? Back to her apartment to seek cover with Inga and Sven? But that would be the first place he'd look, and she didn't want to visit her problems onto them. Maybe she could head to the mountains and bury herself deep in the bush?

'Don't even think about it, Princess.'

She looked back. 'Think about what?'

'About running away.'

'Who said I was thinking about running away?'

Did she imagine the tweak of his lips, or was it just the crease in the corners as he pressed them tightly together?

'The doors are locked. You're not going anywhere.'

'I accept.'

'Excuse me?'

'I don't intend going anywhere, either. So glad you finally agree.'

He voiced a word that bore more than a slight resemblance to a curse. 'We've established you're not coming quietly, Princess. But I need you to accept that you are coming.'

'And you, Mr Mylonakos,' she said, abandoning all attempts at being placatory, 'need to accept that I'm not.'

'Princess...'

'No. I will not go with you. I refuse to go with you.'

He sighed. 'Yes, so you said.'

'Then why don't you listen to me?'

'Because you're not safe here. You're not safe anywhere on the planet until you're safely returned to Rubanestein.'

'I'm not safe in Rubanestein! Why can't you get that through your head? Or are you a fan of forced marriages? Is that what this is about?'

'Princess—'

'Princess nothing. What if it was your sister? Would you be happy to marry her off to some creep to settle someone else's gambling debts?'

His eyes were bleak. 'My sister is dead.' His voice was low and thick. Gravel over pain.

Oh. Her jibe about him having a sister was meant to be nothing more than a prompt, a search for empathy if there was any empathy to be found inside the man. She hadn't expected to find tragedy instead.

'I'm so sorry.'

He shook his head, as if trying to shake away her words. 'Don't be. It was a long time ago. It's not your fault.'

'I wasn't apologising. I'm sorry for your loss.'

'Good to know,' he said, perfunctorily, the car pulling into a driveway.

Her eyes opened wide as she realised where she was. 'You're staying here?' She'd only been on the island a few days, but it was long enough to know that Capella Lodge was one of the premier accommodation providers on the island. And one of the most expensive. 'You must have some expense account. How much is my brother paying you?'

He looked skywards as he unclipped his seat belt.

'Nowhere near enough,' she said. 'I get it.'

His head swivelled around, and she could see in his

eyes that she'd answered her own question. She shrugged as she slipped her own seat belt from her shoulders. 'You should have asked for more.'

He carried her bag into a suite that was decorated in a calming palette of navy blue and white, broken by cool timber trims and furniture.

'Your bedroom is upstairs,' he said. 'I sleep down here.'

'In case I try to run away?'

'You can try, but what would be the point? There's nowhere to run on this island and there's no way you'll get off it.'

'Isn't that what I already told you?'

'Sure, but if I have to watch you, I'd rather you were here, sleeping upstairs, than at your apartment with me sleeping on your floor waiting for you to jump out the window at any moment.'

She looked around, taking in the décor. It was a world apart from her humble cabin. The suite oozed luxury, the floor-to-ceiling-length windows drinking in the view. In a break in the cloud, a glimmer of moonlight, there was no missing the shadow of the twin mountains looming ominously over them, while the fronds of the kentia palms provided the musical score, chattering and clapping in the breeze. The wind was rising, but that had been expected given the route of the cyclone passing to the north.

'I guess it might be a fraction more comfortable.' She turned to him. 'Now, about my shift tomorrow evening...'

* * *

He shook his head. 'Not happening. We're leaving tomorrow.'

'It's just one day,' she pleaded. 'Twenty-four little hours. Where's the harm in that?'

'No chance,' he said. 'With that cyclone brewing off the coast, I'm not risking the airport closing and getting stuck here on the island with no way off.'

'I heard it's changed direction and veered away. Please, let me work this one shift. And then I'll come with you.'

Like hell she'd come with him. When she was no doubt already thinking of a plan to get away and continue her little escapade somewhere else.

She must have read the doubt in his eyes. 'I'm not planning on running away again, if that's what you're worried about. I just don't want to let my friends down. They were good enough to give me a job when I had no experience, and I won't leave them in the lurch, just because you have an overblown sense of responsibility.'

He didn't bother responding. She wasn't going to listen anyway.

'For goodness' sake,' she went on, trying to make him see reason and bend even just a little. 'It's just one more day. Where's the problem with that?'

There was a problem. No, there were two. The first problem was that the Prince had been informed, and Theo would not risk losing the Princess. Not after she'd already embarrassed him and his firm by evading discovery for so long.

The second was more disturbing. There was something about the Princess—something that set alarm bells ringing under his skin. It was bad enough that she was attractive. But he didn't need to know how well she felt in his arms. He knew she was a danger to him—someone he needed to keep his distance from. The sooner he was rid of her, the better.

The Princess was impatient for his reply. 'Check out the weather radar if you don't believe me. The island isn't in the path of the storm.'

He didn't answer. Simply turned away to stash his bag in his room.

'Please,' she said, chasing after him. 'It's important to me. Don't make me let them down.'

He turned back on a sigh. 'It's not up for discussion, Princess. Now, how about you go upstairs and wash out whatever the hell that cacophony of colour is that you've got going on in your hair?'

Izzy was beyond frustrated. She stepped into the rainforest shower and tilted her head under the cascade of water. She didn't need shampoo at first, the chalk washed freely from her hair, turning the floor of the shower stall into a crazy shifting kaleidoscope.

As the colour bleached away, Izzy felt like she was losing the identity she'd been so enjoying. The freewheeling backpacker adventurer she'd been pretending to be was being washed away, and more and more it felt like she was being forced back into her previous life. The life of the Princess Isabella. Bound by protocols. Restricted by rules.

Sold to the highest bidder.

And her captor thought nothing of forcing her back to the hell-hole she'd escaped. And yet she was no minor who'd run off in a snit. She was an adult. And if there were rogue actors out there who were after her for their own gain, as he'd claimed, maybe it was preferable to risk her future with them. She'd successfully avoided her pursuers until now, and why shouldn't she keep avoiding them? There was no safety awaiting her in Rubanestein.

It was clear she was going to have to come up with a new strategy. Dealing with Theo was like dealing with a block of granite. The man didn't respond to reason—he had not one ounce of empathy in his entire body. He thought she was lying, he thought she was confecting her reason for running. He had clearly drunk her brother's Kool-Aid. That, or he was being paid so much that his head wasn't about to be turned. Whatever the reason, clearly, he wasn't about to change his mind any time soon.

Which meant she had to up her game.

If she didn't, she'd be on that plane to Sydney tomorrow and heading back to Rubanestein and a fate and a future she couldn't bear. All she needed was a plan.

From the far edges of her mind random thoughts and possibilities drifted in and out of view, until like jigsaw pieces, some of them fitted together, forming a scheme that she would never before have considered, let alone dared. But these were extraordinary times. Desperate times. And as someone very wise a very long time ago said, desperate times called for desperate measures.

The only question was, was she brave enough to carry out her crazy plan?

CHAPTER SIX

I⊤ WAS A summer trip to the beach, a rare escape from their landlocked village for Theo's hard-working family. The sun shone in a sky of endless blue, the golden sand warm beneath their feet. Together the family built a sandcastle, decorating the walls with shells and digging a moat around it, along with a canal to let in the incoming waves.

Theo's younger sister gave squeals of delight as every wave after wave flowed in, filling the moat surrounding their sandcastle, before draining back into the sea. And when that novelty wore off, Theo and his sister played in the shallows, following schools of tiny fish while their parents took a break under a tent set up on the shore.

It was a perfect summer day.

The change came almost imperceptibly at first. A subtle shift in the weather, the breeze changing direction and turning gusty, stirring gentle waves into whitecaps. Laughter from swimmers turned to whoops, some of delight, some of shock as the waves built.

Theo's father was the first in their family to react. 'Theo, Helena,' he called, rising from his chair, 'it's time to come out.'

Theo agreed. They were still only in the shallows, but

a sudden undertow was sucking at his legs. He turned to relay the message to his sister in case she hadn't heard, when he saw a wave break behind her, knocking her off her feet and tumbling her into the wash.

'Helena!' he screamed, bracing himself against the crashing wave before surging through the water to reach his sister. Until just a moment before Helena had been a scant few feet away. But a few feet might well have been light years away. The sea was now a mess of white froth and tumbled sand, his sister nowhere to be seen. The next wave caught him unawares, sending him sprawling.

He felt something brush past his arm—*Helena!*—and he made a desperate lunge for her, but she slipped away, sucked in the backwash. He emerged, gasping from the water, catching a glimpse of his sister being dragged out.

He struck out in his novice freestyle, battling to keep his head above water, struggling to keep her in his sights, desperate to reach her. *Frantic.*

'Helena!' he cried.

But despite his calls and his efforts, he couldn't reach her. He couldn't find her.

He couldn't save her...

'Shh, it's okay.'

He was suddenly aware of the warm press of hands at his shoulders. He was aware of the soothing voice through the pain of his loss. A calming voice that made no sense. It was at odds with his memory—of his father pulling him half-drowned from the sea, laying him on the sand where Theo had retched his stomach out, as much from the seawater he'd swallowed as the knowledge that he'd failed his sister.

'It's okay.' The words permeated the thickness in his

mind, yet in an accent that didn't sound like anyone he knew. Not his father who'd plucked him from the sea. A woman, yet not his mother.

Sophia, he thought. It made no sense but it had to be Sophia. Who else could it be but his wife saying soothing words, blotting out memories of the beach tragedy as she had always done? And the nightmare receded, his jagged breathing eased, as he let himself drift at the comforting stroke of her hands on his arms, at her calming perfume coiling into his senses.

Until something snagged with the sensuality of his dream. A hairline crack in the perfection that jarred.

Because Sophia's perfume had been heady and sensual, rich with the spices of the silk route.

Whereas this scent—this scent was citrus and fresh.

And Sophia?

Sophia was gone.

And what started as a hairline crack grew into a fracture, shattering his dreamlike state and jolting him into wakefulness.

His eyes snapped open. It was dark but he was fully awake. He saw her face—*Isabella's face*—close to his, as she murmured soothing words and heaven turned into hell.

He roared into the darkened room, rearing upright in the bed, pulling the sheet over his body with one hand, seizing one of her wrists with the other. He snapped on the bedside light. She whimpered as she scuttled from the bed as far as she could, as far as she could go with one wrist ensnared. 'You frightened me.'

The colour in her cheeks was high, her hair was mussed from sleep, and had her lips always been that plump and inviting? Her candy-striped pyjama shorts showed off her smooth-skinned legs. Her tiny lace camisole revealed too much the fullness of her breasts, not to mention the pointed peaks of her nipples. He tore his eyes away, half wishing he'd left the light off so he couldn't notice.

'What the hell are you doing?'

'You scared me.'

'Tell me what you were playing at?'

'I didn't mean to wake you.'

'Answer the question!'

'You were having a nightmare. You were calling out. I was worried about you.' She looked down at her wrist, still encircled by his long-fingered hand. 'Are you going to let me go or are you going to hold onto me all night.'

He was in two minds, his thoughts in turmoil. All he knew was that his dream had turned into a living nightmare, and he couldn't get out of bed. He was naked beneath the sheet, memories of Sophia turning him hard. Finding a woman in his bed wearing scant clothing when he was in such a state was next-level hell.

She licked her lips, as if his hesitation was in her favour, her eyes traversing his naked chest as if she was sizing him up. 'Because if you want me to stay…?'

He flung her hand away.

'Don't you realise how dangerous that was coming into my bedroom—where it could have ended up? What it might have cost you?'

'I was worried about you,' she said, a challenge clear in her voice. 'You were calling out.'

He glared at her, hating her for reminding him of the loss of his younger sister. Hating himself more for letting her witness his weakness. And then there was his mad decision to sleep commando. He'd expected the Princess to try to escape—he'd improvised alarms on the doors and windows in case she tried to make a run for it. The last thing he'd expected was for her to ambush him in his own bedroom. He growled at his lack of foresight.

'You acted foolishly, Princess.'

'What else was I supposed to do—leave you to shout the house down?'

'And if I had been less ethical and found you in my bed and taken advantage of you, how would you be feeling now?'

She blinked, her lips curling into a wicked smile. 'Satisfied, I hope.'

'*Vlammeni!*' he said, hitting the heel of one hand against his brow. If the dossier he'd been provided was accurate, the Princess had fled the castle an innocent. He didn't need to know why or how—he didn't much care—all he cared about was bringing her home in the same state. 'You know nothing about what happens between a man and a woman. Your actions were reckless. I expected more of you, Princess.'

She flung back her head, setting the ends of her hair in motion. Platinum-blonde hair now that she'd washed the colour from it. For once it wasn't tied back in a ponytail, allowing the waves to dance around her face, the curled tendrils, still damp, brushing over her chest, over the full breasts that swelled and swayed under her camisole. He swallowed. He really hadn't needed to notice that. He averted his eyes.

'Oh, I know more than you think I do.'

'The hell you do!' He was angry with her. But he was

angrier with himself for noticing her hair. Her breasts. And he was angry that she no longer looked like a recalcitrant teenager now that she'd washed the veritable rainbow from her hair, because now she looked like a woman.

All woman.

'What do you think I've been doing these last few weeks? There have been plenty of men willing to educate me. There was this cool surfer guy called Luke from Bondi, who had sun-bleached hair and big blue eyes, and his abs—OMG his abs! You should have seen them. And then there was the Spanish barista, Mateo, from the coffee bar around the corner from Erin's apartment. He was seriously hot. Oh, but then—'

He held out one hand to stop her. So much for getting her home unharmed and unscathed. But if the Princess had made the most of her freedom and was no longer the innocent she'd been painted, he didn't need to know. He didn't want to know. 'But then nothing! I don't want to hear this.'

'I'm just saying I know more—'

It was his turn to cut her off. 'And I said I don't want to hear it. Save it for your girlfriends back home.'

Her chin jutted up and out. 'And just when am I going to have a chance to talk to these so-called friends of mine? Rafael will lock me up like a prisoner the moment you deliver me back into his clutches. Right up until the time he trusses me up like a turkey and sends me off to marry his crony.'

'You're being melodramatic again, Princess.'

'I'm being honest! This will happen! Do you know how hard it was for me to escape the palace? I might as

well have been under house arrest. It was a miracle I
managed to get away.'

'How did you get away?'

She shrugged. 'I pretended to be one of the cleaners,
heading home to the village at the end of the day. All the
women were wearing shawls. Nobody at the gate both-
ers to look at ID on the way out.'

Theo nodded. So security at the palace had been lax.
So different from the story that he'd been told of her
being spirited out the palace by a gang of enablers. He
imagined that someone would have paid for that lapse
and that things would be very different now.

'He'll make it impossible for me to so much as breathe
once you take me home. Is that what you want for me?
To be made a prisoner in my own country before he
marries me off to his creepy friend. At least here, I'm
free to make my own choices and my own friends.' She
shrugged. 'And at least I had the chance to meet a few
decent men while I was in Australia.'

He shook his head. He'd heard enough. He had a job
to do, and he intended to do it. 'Get back to your room.
Get some sleep.' One of them might as well sleep tonight,
and he knew damned well it wasn't going to be him.

She tilted her head to one side, her expression turning coquettish as she ran her teeth over her bottom lip.
Her full, pink, bottom lip. 'Are you really sure you want
me to go?'

'Get out!'

She straightened her shoulders and flicked back her
hair and damn if the action didn't make her breasts sway
again. 'Then I'll go. But I'll keep an ear out in case you
need me again.'

He growled. 'Go!' Wishing she would.

He watched her leave. God, he could have had her and ruined his business in the process. But still he was unable to tear his eyes from the low-slung shorty pyjamas swaying with her hips. She was trying to be provocative; he knew that. She was trying to get under his skin. He pulled on a pair of boxer shorts—he wasn't getting surprised again—lay down and punched his pillow.

The trouble was, she was succeeding.

But tomorrow.

Tomorrow he would be done with her and tomorrow couldn't come soon enough.

So that had been a revelation. Izzy padded slowly up the stairs to her room, her senses still buzzing at what had transpired. She'd been lying in bed for what seemed like hours, trying to build up the courage to sneak down into Theo's room and see if he might welcome her company. But what had seemed a good plan in theory, was proving harder to carry out in real life.

She'd been kidding herself dreaming up her crazy plan. What did she really know about seducing men?

The first time she'd heard Theo cry out, she'd thought she'd imagined it and it must be just another sound generated by the winds, but then it came again, and again. Sounds of distress and panic and insufferable pain, and it had been compassion that had led her feet down the stairs. She'd stood at his open door a few moments to see if he'd calm naturally, but he twisted in his sheets, producing sounds like a wounded animal.

She knew better than to wake someone having a nightmare, but she could soothe him. She drew closer, sitting on the side of the bed, murmuring words of comfort, stroking his fevered skin. Firm skin over corded muscles. Her fingers drank him in, even as she continued to whisper soft words. A sliver of light through the blinds silhouetted his body, highlighting his strong chest and flat belly leading to the tangled sheet below. And she'd wondered—what if she had found the courage to descend the stairs? Could her plan have worked?

Theo was calming, his movements less frantic, his breathing steadier. 'It's okay,' she'd whispered one more time close to his ear, and suddenly all hell had broken loose.

He'd been angry. He hadn't welcomed her with open arms. But he hadn't been unaffected by her either.

And that was encouraging.

Izzy wasn't about to give up her plans to get Theo onside just yet.

CHAPTER SEVEN

THEO SAT AT the dining room table nursing both a thick head and a third mug of black coffee. Caffeine had never been so essential, and if he could find a way to take it intravenously, he would. He'd not allowed himself to more than doze the rest of the night, afraid to fall asleep while on princess watch. He didn't trust her an inch. He didn't trust her assurances that she would come with him. He didn't believe that she wouldn't try to run the first chance she got. The sooner he got her on the plane out of here the better. And then maybe, once they'd got to Sydney and she was on board the private jet that would whisk them back to Rubanestein—maybe then he could get some sleep.

Until then, coffee—and a bucket load of it—would have to suffice.

He heard her light footfall skipping down the stairs before she emerged into the room.

'Good morning,' she said, looking bright-eyed and way too pleased with herself for his liking. She was still wearing the shortie pyjamas, but at least she'd had the good sense this morning to add a robe. Because she was cold? At least he could thank the weather for something.

Although she might have thought to tie the robe around her waist instead of leaving it undone and exposing her legs. He looked away.

'Morning,' he answered, rising from the table to pick up the plunger of coffee he'd made ten minutes earlier. Because as far as he was concerned, there was little good about it. He'd already heard the news, that the storm had changed track again, and that there was a chance the airport would be closed today. Which meant at least another twenty-four hours in this woman's presence. AKA, disaster. 'Coffee?'

He was already pouring it when he heard, 'You might be my captor, but you don't have to wait on me.'

'You're not my captive,' he said. 'And no, I don't have to wait on you. I was merely being polite.' He put the cup down in front of her and went to stand with his back against the kitchen benchtop. 'There's bread in the toaster waiting for you. The milk's in the fridge. The sugar's in the dish over there. Help yourself.'

'Thank you, but I take my coffee black.'

He growled under his breath. He didn't like that they had something in common, even if it was as simple as how they took their coffee.

'You don't sound very happy,' she said. 'Didn't you sleep well?'

When he didn't answer, she continued, 'I had the best sleep.'

A burst of rain lashed the windows. The building seemed to rattle on its foundations.

She looked at the windows, to where the palm fronds bent and swayed in the wind and rain. 'Is the storm getting worse?'

'Looks like it. That's why we're getting out of here while we still can.'

She looked at him, all trace of smugness or smarts gone from her face, and what he was left with was cold hard determination. 'I'm not going back.'

He sighed. 'Princess, face the facts. You are going back.'

'No,' she said, jumping from her chair. 'I will not. Not if it means getting married off to someone my brother chose so he can get his debts paid off.'

'You're a princess. You have duties.'

'I'm a woman, first and foremost. I'm not my brother's chattel to be sold off to whoever can offer him the most. It's wrong. It's barbaric—and if you can't see that, then you're just as much a barbarian and misogynist as he is.'

He was losing his patience. There was no arguing with this woman, no way to make her see sense. 'If I were a barbarian, as you say, things would have ended very differently last night. And you wouldn't be looking quite so smug right now.'

She angled her head, as if weighing up his words. 'Oh, I don't know. I might be looking even more smug.'

He growled again, tossing the dregs of his coffee into the sink, wishing he could rid himself of this troublesome princess just as easily. 'Get dressed,' he said.

'Why? We're not going anywhere. The flight isn't for hours.'

He wanted her out of those shortie pyjamas. No, that was wrong. He wanted her out of those pyjamas, *and* into something thoroughly more all-encompassing. But he was sick of arguing with her. 'Just do it,' he said, and stalked from the room.

God, if it wasn't bad enough that he'd been awake since she'd ambushed him, afraid to fall asleep in case she tried something again. Afraid that next time he might not be strong enough to turn her down. It had been eight years since Sophia had died, and despite plenty of women trying, he'd felt nothing for any of them. But last night that had changed. Last night he'd wanted a woman.

This woman.

The wrong woman, in every way.

And yet still he hungered for her. Found himself almost regretting the fact he'd come to his senses before the unthinkable had happened. The unthinkable—and yet—the very much *wantable*.

What was that about?

Unless his body was finally rebelling about the long drought that had followed Sophia's death? A shame, if that were so, to randomly pick this woman to awaken his desire. She was a rescue. Attraction wasn't an option.

He heard her footfall going up the stairs. At last. He returned to the kitchen and helped himself to more coffee, and just as quickly drained the cup as he paced the suite and watched the rain coming in bursts against the windows. He was going to need all the caffeine he could get before he got on that plane.

He heard the pad of her bare feet coming down the stairs and turned, relieved to know she'd be out of those shortie pyjamas at last. Except... 'What the hell? I thought I told you to get dressed.'

She held out her arms and looked down at herself, as if he were crazy. 'I am dressed.'

Not in his book. She was wearing a bikini, a tiny bikini that left little to the imagination. It was strapless and red, with a little ruffle at the top of the bandeau. If it had ruffles anywhere else, he didn't want to know. And he'd thought her shortie pyjamas were provocative. He closed his eyes and sent up a silent prayer for strength.

'Where do you think you're going in that?'

'I thought I'd take a swim.'

'Outside? Where it's blowing a gale?'

'But it's not cold, Lord Howe Island is a subtropical island so it's not cold, is it? Just a bit windy. And it would be a crime to waste a plunge pool like that, don't you think?'

He didn't think. He couldn't right now. Instead, he rubbed his whiskered jaw with his hand. He needed to shave. He needed more coffee. He needed this woman gone. Out of his sight. Out of his life.

'Go then,' he said, his voice sounding rough and gravelly, unrecognisable even to his own ears. 'Go have your swim.'

She smiled and gave a little curtsy. 'I wasn't actually asking your permission, but thank you anyway.'

He didn't dare look at her as she walked to the door, didn't want to see the sway of her hips or the curves of her body so open to his gaze, didn't want to be reminded of how close he'd been last night. But when the door opened and the storm front gusted in, his eyes found her paused in the open doorframe. For a moment she hesitated, as if she were having second thoughts. But then her shoulders lifted, and she pushed into the swirling air and tugged the door closed behind her.

It was wild outside. The wind swirled around her, tugging at her hair, threatening to blow her sideways at times, but no way was she retreating. Not until she'd wound him in so many knots that he couldn't untie himself. She lowered herself into the plunge pool, exaggerating the sway of her hips as she made her way one slow step at a time. She could feel his eyes on her. She could feel their heat.

And she was determined to stoke it.

What was wrong with the man?

She knew he hadn't been unaffected by her.

And he was all man. So strong. So firm. Even in sleep his body was hard, his belly taut with muscle. And she hadn't imagined the impact of his heat. One touch and her senses had surged, like she'd plugged herself into a battery pack and felt the energy flare inside her. This man was neither stone nor metal. No robot. This man was made of flesh and blood, the same as her—and yet so very different.

It was almost a shame that he'd woken before she'd had the chance to experience more. But even in her limited experience with men and with this man in particular, she recognised that she'd planted the seeds of desire, and now it was her job to nurture them. If only she could get him onside. If only she could create some kind of rapport between them that wasn't based on his job description and her situation. Then she might have a chance to reason with the man.

What else could she do?

Which was exactly why she was here.

She lay in the pool, her arms beside her on the edge, her legs kicking the surface of the spa as they floated free. The wind buffeted her face, tugging at her hair. She didn't care. The water temperature was perfect, and the wind was the least of her problems. She wondered instead at the words Theo had uttered in his sleep. Wondered what would have happened if he had tumbled her over and finished what she had begun. Her body had been trembling with excitement, she'd felt herself pulsing in places she didn't know could pulse. He was big. And she might be inexperienced sexually, but she knew enough to know that size mattered. Instinctually she knew that size *had* to matter. What must it feel like, to have *that* inside you? To feel that move inside you. Even now the memories of last night had her belly quivering anew, triggering an ache deep between her thighs that she didn't understand or know how to ease. Only that it had something to do with Theo.

She needed more time to explore these new sensations. She wanted more time. But there was no more time. Today she would leave the island, and he would take her back to Rubanestein and into the grasping clutches of her brother Rafael.

If her brother got his way, she'd be married off to Count Lorenzo di Stasio before she'd got off the plane. Love would never come into it. Money ruled her brother's life. Cruelty ruled her so-called fiancé's.

She shuddered. She didn't like any of her brother's so-called friends. She never had. From the time she'd been old enough to notice, they'd watched her with hungry eyes, exchanging secret smiles.

While her father had been alive, she'd been protected. She'd been safe. But her father was gone, and now her brother thought he was master of the universe. Master of her destiny.

To him she was nothing more than a piece of meat, to

be sold to the highest bidder. And her not-so-dear brother had done exactly that.

She would not go back.

But if worst came to the worst and this man forced her to do exactly that, she couldn't afford to let her brother win. Not entirely. He might ultimately succeed in marrying her off to the count, but she wouldn't let anyone she didn't want to marry take the one thing she'd protected for so long. She might be up for sale, but she refused to throw in her virginity as a bonus.

So, what choice did she have? Why shouldn't she take matters into her own hands? Why shouldn't her first time be with someone *she* chose? She'd said no to both Luke and Mateo. She'd turned them down because she hadn't given up on the dream that she might marry for love and the man that she married would be her first. Because she'd been saving herself. But time was rapidly running out for her to make a choice of her own.

She knew Theo wasn't unmoved last night. He might have been half asleep, but he had responded to her presence and her touch like he wanted it. Like he welcomed it.

And if she had to decide who to give her virginity to between Theo and the Count de Lorenzo, there was no contest.

Sure, it wouldn't be the way she'd always wanted it to be. She'd always wanted the whole fairy tale. She wanted to fall in love and marry someone who loved her too, the way her mother and father had loved each other. She wanted her first time to be with the man she would spend the rest of her life with.

The wind tugged at her hair, sending ends flicking against her closed eyes. She turned over, resting her head on her crossed arms, catching a glimpse of Theo watching her through the window before he darted out of view.

A frisson shivered down her spine, setting nerves strumming and making her toes curl in the water. Even just a glimpse of him set the space between her thighs tingling. So, maybe her first time wouldn't be with the man she would spend the rest of her life with, but at least it would be with a man who set her senses alight. And clearly, the seeds she had planted were sprouting. She would be the one to choose who her first time would be. And it wouldn't be so bad. She could do a whole lot worse than a man who stirred her senses.

She sighed. Reckless, Theo had called her, and so what that he was right? There was a time for reckless, and with time in short supply, there was no better time for reckless than now.

She just had to work out how and when.

Theo rubbed the back of his neck with one hand as he strode the length of the apartment. He shouldn't have jumped when she'd caught him watching.

It certainly wasn't that he wanted to watch her. Especially not when she was wearing nothing more than a few square inches of fabric that only served to reveal more than they hid. It was a form of torture she was subjecting him to, and he was in no doubt that was her absolute intention. Her curves—her ample breasts, her tiny waist and the sweet flare to her hips—reminded him so much of both what he'd experienced so briefly while in dreamland last night and what he'd missed and hungered for so long.

In any event, it wasn't like he'd just been watching her,

because naturally he'd been anxious about the weather too. The twin mountains of Lidgbird and Gower were now shrouded in a donut of cloud that ominously circled their peaks while the wind thrashed at the palms and the foliage below.

The latest he'd heard the airport was still open and flights today were still expected to go ahead, but he wouldn't relax until they were on the plane and both safely Sydney bound.

But none of that was the real issue.

The real issue was that he wasn't about to risk her running again. He turned back to the window. As difficult as it was, he had no choice but to watch her.

That was all.

It was another twenty minutes before the Princess decided that she'd had enough of flaunting herself in the plunge pool. Finally, she emerged. It was a relief and yet it just proved another set of challenges, because the door blasted open as she entered the room dripping wet. Of course, he thought, teeth gritted, she hadn't bothered taking a towel let alone putting on her robe.

'Go and get yourself showered and packed,' he yelled against the wind, as he battled to close the door. 'As far as we know the flight is still on.'

'But I'm dripping water,' she said, clutching her arms around her waist, her robe trailing uselessly from her hands.

The door snapped closed. 'Then run,' he said, without turning to look at her. He was fed up with her antics.

Thirty minutes later, he was zipping up his duffel bag when above the wild weather, he heard someone beating on the door. 'Who is it?' the Princess said, appearing down the stairs. His gaze flicked over her attire. It was a relief to see her finally wearing something more appropriate— jeans and loafers with a soft knit top.

He held up a hand to shush her. He opened the door a crack. It was Tom Parker outside, bringing the message Theo least wanted to hear. Theo cursed, forcing closed the door after the message had been delivered. He shouldn't have been surprised. The wind had been building all morning, the squalls coming more and more furiously, but still the news was like a body blow. The cyclone had deviated closer to the island. It was expected to track away eventually, but for today, the news was grim. The airport was closed. There would be no flights in or out today.

He turned, his face grave and no doubt betraying his disappointment. 'It seems like you got your way, Princess. The airport is closed. We won't be leaving today.'

It galled him that she looked halfway delighted. 'Oh, that is a shame. I mean, you must be itching to get back to your work. Hunting down international criminal masterminds and all that.'

'I am looking forward to completing this case, yes.'

'So sad, I know how much you were looking forward to be done with me.'

He ground his teeth. 'I can wait a day,' he said, even as his eyes stung from lack of sleep. 'I've waited this long already.'

Her eyes suddenly brightened. 'Then—if we're not leaving, I can work my shift tonight, right?'

Theo pressed thumb and forefinger to the bridge of his nose. He needed sleep desperately. He needed even more not to be bothered with this undeserving princess. But if he could grab a decent meal while keeping an eye on her, the evening might not be a total waste.

'I'll be watching you,' he said. 'Every move you make.'

'Oh,' she said with a smile and a coquettish hitch of one shoulder, 'If you insist. Well, I guess I'd better go get unpacked again.'

'Don't get too excited,' he growled. 'This delay is for a day. Twenty-four hours. Don't bother unpacking everything. I'm sure we'll be on our way tomorrow.'

'We'll see,' she said.

Theo watched her go.

Sure she was happy about their departure being delayed, he got that, but she was almost too happy. Almost flirtatious. What was that about?

Bottom line, after last night's little escapade, he didn't trust her an inch.

'So, what would you like to do today?'

The Princess was standing and leaning her elbows on the kitchen counter, snacking on an apple. Theo didn't like her stance. Mostly because of the way her knit top clung to her curves, accentuating her breasts and then the scoop to her waist, and then that shapely derriere jutting out behind.

Not that he was about to protest the way she was standing and let her know how she affected him. Instead, he said, 'What are you talking about? Haven't you looked outside?'

Her gaze flickered to the windows. 'Sure, it's blowy.

But do you really want to waste this bonus time on the island?'

He snorted. 'Bonus time. That's one way to put it.'

'But it is. Do you realise Lord Howe Island is one of Tripadvisor's top ten places to visit in the entire world?'

'And your point is?'

'And you would have had, what?—if this weather event hadn't intervened—just twenty-four hours to experience the island's magic. At least now you have the chance to experience more of what the island has to offer.'

He glanced out the window again. The wind was mad, palm trees lashed from side to side, their fronds buffeting and slapping together in the wind. 'What exactly did you have in mind, Princess? A climb around the cliffs and up to the heights of Mt Gower? A glass-bottom boat tour of the coral reef? Or maybe a scenic flight over the island?'

She put her hands on her hips, slowly shaking her tilted head. 'You are such a fun person, you know that?'

He moved his head from side to side. Slowly. Deliberately. 'I'm not here to have fun. I'm here to do a job, Princess. And I fully intend to carry it out.'

Her smile slid away, her eyes dropped. His words had hit the mark and he'd just reminded her what the end goal was.

Good.

He didn't need the taunting. It wasn't like he didn't know what fun was. He remembered fun. He remembered good times.

Even if none recently.

The fun times, the good times, had ended when Sophia had. When he looked back, he couldn't think of any good times he'd had since then.

Now he didn't look for fun.

Instead, what he'd found in its place was the satisfaction he'd taken from his work. Reuniting kidnapped children with their desperate families. Finding lost and missing and amnesiac adults who appeared to have fallen off the face of the earth without a trace.

He'd been too busy seeking justice to look for fun. Too busy trying to atone for what had happened.

Too busy.

The Princess huffed into the silence. 'Then what are we supposed to do? I'm going to be stuck here in this apartment with you for hours.'

He had no sympathy. He was going to be stuck here in this apartment with her for hours too. Did she really think it was going to be a cakewalk for him?

With one arm he gestured towards a stacked bookshelf. 'Try reading a book,' he said, sitting at the dining table attempting to find a shred of wireless signal to log into his office. He needed to contact Prince Rafael to let him know their return was delayed, and it was frustrating that there was a part of the world that didn't boast superfast Wi-Fi capabilities, and that was where he was now. Whereas Lord Howe Island's isolation had proved advantageous when he'd been tracking down the Princess, it was also proving to be a curse. It was all well and good to sell the island's lack of connectivity as the perfect excuse to chill out and wind down, but when you were trying to work, it was a positive handicap.

Eventually he heard the Princess huff. A glance of his eyes was all it needed to tell him that she was walking towards the bookshelf. Then somehow, he didn't even need to glance to know that she stayed there a minute or two, selecting and rejecting the options—his senses told him that, seemingly becoming hyper aware where this woman was concerned—before apparently finding something that caught her interest, taking it back to the sofa and flopping down on her back to read it.

At last. He let go a breath he hadn't realised he'd been holding. Feeling relief. At least for now. Finally, she'd found something to take her mind off their circumstances. And at least now he could think about something other than a hovering bundle of platinum-blonde nervous tension pacing around the apartment.

All too sexy platinum-blonde nervous tension. He felt that tension vibrate through him, almost like she'd emitted it purely to mess with his nerve endings.

Outside the clouds finally unleashed the promised flood of rain, adding to the cacophony of noise battering the roof and windows. Wild. Primal.

Elemental.

Like the friction building up between them. An attraction unwanted and yet seemingly unavoidable. An attraction coupled with confusion. It made no sense to him.

He looked up to see what was left of the view of the mountains disappear in a cascade of grey. So, the forecasters had been right about the weather worsening? Maybe he should be glad the authorities had closed the airport and their tiny plane wasn't currently trying to struggle its way through this weather.

Then again—he glanced over at the Princess, looking like she was trying to get involved with whatever she was reading. He was relieved she'd stopped pacing. Though that hadn't stopped the gnawing in his gut or the uncomfortable bristling awareness of her. She had one arm behind her head, holding the book with her other hand, and perched up on her chest. Her fine knitted top clung to her curves, showing off the pronounced line where her ribcage ended, before sweeping down to her flat belly to meet her slim fitted jeans. She'd kicked off her shoes and now the nearest leg was bent, showing off the line of her under leg from knee to the sweet curve of her butt where it rested on the sofa.

He dragged his eyes away. He knew he should be relieved she'd finally stopped complaining. But it would be a damned sight easier if the Princess didn't look the way she did. *Theos.* He'd tracked her to the island and found her the first day, only for a simple extraction to be stymied by the weather.

Why couldn't anything be simple?

He turned back to his search to find a wisp of internet to see if his enquiry about drilling down further into the Prince's gambling habits had turned up anything but came up a blank.

Damn it. Maybe it would have been preferable to take their chances with the weather after all.

Not an hour later she sighed theatrically and tossed her book aside. She got up from the sofa and again started pacing the rain-lashed windows back and forth like a caged lion. Then she suddenly stopped, hands on hips, staring out at the palms thrashing in the cyclonic winds and teeming rain.

'I'm bored,' she stated bluntly.

He didn't bother looking up. He knew exactly what she was doing. 'How's the book?'

'Didn't I just tell you? I'm bored. It's boring. Aren't you bored?'

He was frustrated, yes. Annoyed at the delay, certainly. Impatient to get this woman back to Rubanestein and out of his life, hell yes! And then there was that niggling discomfort in his gut that she seemed to somehow trigger just by her mere presence.

But bored didn't factor. Not where this woman was concerned. Not when this woman was proving to be one surprise after another. A princess who'd found work as a waitress and who seemed to enjoy it so much that she was insisting to do one last shift. A princess who'd traded gowns and tiaras for flip-flops.

A princess who'd sneaked into his bedroom last night in an attempt to—what? Seduce him? So he'd be swayed to relent and not to take her home? Whatever other motive could she have had?

She was also a princess who looked too damned good from the rear for his liking. No, that wasn't right. A princess who looked too damned good from any angle and any way you looked at her.

Why the hell did she have to stand there in front of the window that way? It gave him the perfect view of her hourglass figure.

'Maybe,' he said, his voice huskier than he'd intended, 'you picked the wrong book.'

She shook her head, setting her blonde waves dancing. She lifted one hand to her hair and smoothed it back. 'Maybe I'm just not in the mood for reading.'

He raised an eyebrow. 'In that case, I see that one of

the bookshelves is overflowing with games. Maybe you could find a deck of cards and amuse yourself that way.'

She suddenly spun around, ignoring the puzzle shelf, before pulling up a chair opposite him at the table. 'How old are you?'

'What?'

'I said I'm bored. So, since we're stuck here together, maybe we could find out more about each other? So, how old are you?'

He shook his head. 'Princess—'

'Oh, that's not fair. I bet my darling brother has provided you an entire dossier on me. I bet you know everything there is to know about me. Birth date, schools I attended, friends I had, shoe size, probably even my dental records. And yet, here I am, knowing next to nothing about you. Or even if you're one of these rogue actors you're supposedly saving me from. Maybe you might try to persuade me a little that you're who you say you are.'

Theo didn't want to admit that it wasn't just her body, it was the sound of her voice that stirred him. Her voice was melodic and elegant, evidence of her principality's Mediterranean connections with its linkages to both France and Italy. Theo also didn't want to admit that the Princess was spot on. Theo had been given all those details and more. 'It's not usual procedure for a recovery expert to divulge details to a recoveree.'

'I doubt I'm your usual "recoveree". But I'd really appreciate those details. I'd like to know who it is who is abducting me. I'd like to know who that man is.'

'I'm not abducting you. I'm taking you home, before something untoward happens to you.'

'Oh, that's right. You're rescuing me before someone

else finds and kidnaps me for whatever nefarious reasons they might have. I forgot.'

Theo closed his laptop and squeezed the bridge of his nose. 'Downplay it all you like, Princess. Just be thankful I found you first.'

'In that case, tell me, who did find me first?'

'I did.'

'And who are you exactly?'

'You know who I am. My name is Theo Mylonakos.'

'And you're a bounty hunter, right?'

He blinked. Slowly. 'I'm a recovery expert.'

'A bounty hunter, I get it.'

He shook his head. He knew of such agents, who prioritised money before the safety of their clients. He had no regard for them. They cluttered up the field, messing with the tracks, getting in the way.

'You mean you're not getting paid? You're doing this as some act of charity?'

'Do you seriously think I'd be putting up with all this—and with you—for free?'

She snorted. 'So, not a bounty hunter. Just in it for the money. That's so much better.'

'If you say so, Princess.'

She sniffed and looked away, and he wondered if she'd been trying to bait him, looking for a bigger reaction. 'So how much did my charming brother pay you? What's the deal?'

'I'm not going to tell you that.'

'What if I offered to pay you more than he did?'

'It doesn't work that way.'

'How does it work?'

'I find you and return you home. That's how it works, Princess. End of story.'

She sat back in her chair, clearly unsatisfied, but any respite didn't last longer than it took to work out her next line of attack.

'So where do you come from? Where were you born?'

'I'm Greek. From a town called Sparta.'

'Sparta? Isn't that the place where they used to train boys to become tough and battle hard and become the best warrior soldiers in Greece?'

'In ancient times, yes.'

He watched her digest that detail, before she added, 'And you're descended from those people. The tough guys of Greece. Is it that warrior mentality that led you to become a bounty hunter—I mean, *"recovery expert"*?'

'No.' His choice to become a recovery expert had its origins in an entirely different sphere. 'My parents are humble orchardists, like their parents and their parents before them. They still live there.'

She nodded, as if summing up his answers. 'And so how old are you? You never said.'

He sighed. 'Is this entirely necessary?'

'No, but I think it's fair, given you probably know details about me down to my shoe size and whether I squeeze toothpaste from the middle or the end of the tube.'

'I'm thirty-four. And no, I don't know how you squeeze your toothpaste. Nor do I particularly care.'

'Ha, but shoe size, you know!'

He pushed his chair back and stood, unable to sit opposite her any longer. This wasn't about him, but she was like a heat-seeking missile and her interrogation was only serving to ramp up his temperature, rendering him a more susceptible target. He moved to the windows, watching the blurred fronds of the palm trees being pelted by the tempest outside. Curse this weather. A glance at his watch told him that they should be in Sydney by now, boarding his private jet and a mere twelve hours or so away from landing in Rubanestein. Whereas right now he was stuck here on this island, with an ungrateful princess who seemed to want to needle him any chance she got and no guarantees that the weather would be any better tomorrow.

'Feeling better?' she asked.

'Define "better".'

She laughed. And he cursed that even her laugh held that accent that seemed to want to coil its way into—not just his hearing—but through his skin and into his bones.

'So, do you have a wife—or a lover—at home?'

He spun around. 'That sounds odd coming from the woman who didn't seem to care last night that she could invade my bedroom and throw herself at me. And only now you think to ask if I was in a relationship.'

'I didn't throw myself at you. I was worried about you.'

He put a hand to his brow. She had a point. It was he who'd had to resist pulling her into the bed and tumbling her beneath him. But it was she who'd put herself into that situation. It was she who'd made his body react.

'So, is there someone special in your life? Are you married?'

His eyes swept the ceiling. 'I was.'

'You were? Separated or divorced?'

He ground his teeth together. 'I'm—a widower.'

She looked sideswiped. 'Oh. I didn't mean—'

Theo didn't wait to hear what it was she didn't mean. He shoved his chair back and stood. 'Now, if you're done with the questions? Because I sure am.'

CHAPTER EIGHT

ISABELLA WATCHED HIM stride from the room. Until her final question, when Theo had snapped, she'd been enjoying the question-and-answer session. The man had to have a weakness somewhere and she was determined to find it. Anything she could glean, she figured, would flesh out more about her captor and had to help her in her quest to escape.

She knew she hadn't learned enough to save her yet, but she now knew more than she had. Theo was a proud Greek, a protector, a bodyguard—and a widower.

That was news.

She wondered about his late wife. What kind of woman could possibly have tamed this cold and hard man-mountain into a loving husband?

And what had happened to her?

Two things were clear—she'd made him angry by raising the topic. And the other more important thing he'd revealed—he wasn't in a current relationship. Because she'd given him every opportunity—surely he would have said if he was? Surely he'd be wanting to deter her from making another attempt at invading his bedroom and throwing herself at him?

And yet he'd not said anything.

Interesting.

Encouraging.

Because he wasn't immune to her. She knew that, from his reaction last night, and from the stolen glances he was so eager to pretend were all about making sure she wasn't trying to run away. She knew that he wouldn't suddenly dart out of view and pretend he wasn't there if he was simply keeping an eye on her to ensure she didn't try to escape.

And now she had one more night.

This time was a gift. Another opportunity to convince Theo to care enough for her that he would listen to her and believe her and wouldn't return her home.

One more night, that's all she had. She just prayed it was enough.

Talk that night at the café was all about the storm. Flights home cancelled. Climbs of Mt Gower, fishing and coral viewing tours cancelled—and the weather outside might be wild, but even with the cancellations, nobody present was complaining about their forced detention on Lord Howe Island. A delay in leaving was a positive. Even if the weather was rubbish, an excuse to extend a holiday was a win. Because nobody really wanted to go home to work and study. The complaints were happily relegated to the holidaymakers on the mainland with bookings to get to the island who were seeing their holiday shrinking by the day.

Nobody seemed glum about their forced retention on Lord Howe Island—apart from Theo.

He sat at table thirty with a dark look of thunder plastered to his face. 'What will it be tonight?' Izzy asked, when she went to take his order. 'The paella again?'

She was sure she almost heard him growl. 'The king-fish,' he said.

'Good choice,' she said. 'And a drink for you, sir? A glass of wine perhaps?'

'Just table water.'

'Wise choice. So that's it?'

He grunted and she spun away back to the kitchen. Millie stopped her behind the bar after she'd delivered the order to the kitchen. 'How's it going with Mr Dream-boat?'

Izzy snorted. She looked back over her shoulder and caught his glare. 'Mr Scowly-Face you mean. Sorry to disappoint you, but nothing's going on.'

'But he's back here tonight and he can't peel his eyes from you.'

She shrugged. 'He's stuck on the island like we all are, and at a guess I'd say he's not happy about it.'

'Do you know he left last night just after you did?'

So, it had been noticed? 'Really?'

'Do you think he's stalking you?'

She shook her head. Not anymore. Theo had already done that. He'd already found her.

'But maybe better safe than sorry. Maybe we should call the police? Get him to have a word.'

She caught one of the diners at one of her tables ges-turing for attention and Izzy, grateful for the change of topic, put her hand to her friend's shoulder. 'Thanks, for worrying about me, but no. There's no need for that. Be-sides, there's a cyclone causing all kinds of problems on the island. I'm sure the police are busy enough as it is.'

She made her way to the table requesting service. She'd thought about appealing to the police, of course, because she could do with another person in her court and to run interference, but she wasn't convinced the police were going to help her. She was no political prisoner seeking asylum. She was a runaway princess who'd gone missing from her country—and if that wasn't enough to raise a goodly number of questions—she'd escaped to the island using someone else's identity. That was going to provide another uncomfortable line of questioning surrounding identity theft. It might have delayed her departure from the island, but in the end, they would probably have handed her back to Theo, happy to see the back of this troublesome princess.

So no, seeking help from the police was no guaranteed way to protect her and prevent whatever Theo had planned.

She had worked out a fallback plan though. If nothing else that she attempted worked between now and their time of departure, she would make a last-ditch attempt at freedom by making a scene at the airport. Hang the uncomfortable consequences, accusations of kidnapping tended to get the attention of security.

Meanwhile she was going to have to find another way around her current problem.

And she was seriously crossing her fingers that she had...

Outside the restaurant the wind howled, buffeting the windows and doors and sending gusts of wet and wild air through the restaurant every time someone attempted to enter or exit. And then the rain started pelting down again, pounding a tattoo on the roof. At the back of the restaurant Theo was protected from all but the mightiest blasts, but still the spray was a bitter reminder of why he was stuck here, on this dot of an island in the middle of the Tasman Sea.

He was so close to closing this deal. He'd managed to hunt down the Princess. He'd located her when nobody else had been able to. How could such a simple thing as the weather be his undoing? And now, instead of delivering the Princess home, as he had been contracted to do, he was stuck here watching his target wait tables.

Wait tables.

A princess.

If he hadn't seen it with his own eyes, he would think it unthinkable. Unimaginable.

And yet, for all he doubted it possible, for all he could see, she was doing a good job. Whatever issues she'd faced during her first shift were clearly behind her. Tonight, the crowd was less frenetic, the guest house with the generator problems having apparently sorted its issues, but still the Princess was run off her feet with the hungry crowd.

She wasn't being precious. She wasn't holding back. She was fully engaged in her work, and with conversations with her tables. More than a few clients, he'd noticed, had ordered the paella. On her recommendation? The diners wouldn't be disappointed. What he'd tasted last night of his meal had been perfection.

She hadn't lied about how good it was. It was no surprise it had reminded her of home.

And again, he had to admit a kind of grudging respect for her. He'd assumed her plea to work her shift tonight was no more than a ploy for her to delay their departure and allow her more time to attempt to escape.

And while there was still an element of truth to that—she'd made it crystal-clear that she didn't want to be removed from her bolt-hole and delivered home and she was going to use any delaying tactic that she could—it was also clear she was good at her job. She might have had a rocky start, as his driver, Tom had alluded to, but clearly, she'd picked up the skills required of her very quickly. Something he hadn't expected of a pampered princess.

She didn't look like any pampered princess now. She looked like any other hard-working waitress, a notebook in her hand, pen behind her ear at the ready.

Why was she here? Why had she run? Her tale of a brother wanting to marry her off was medieval, if not prehistoric. So, was her brother right, that she was envious that he would take the crown when she wasn't able to? A woman who thought she should be the ruler of Rubanestein and yet, here she was, waiting on tables. Hardly the actions of someone who believed she was top of the tree rather than a worker bee. Unless that was part of an act to impress him, to convince him that she was fully invested in her work? He pondered that possibility as he watched her dart between tables, efficiently taking orders, delivering pizzas and paellas, bottles of water and glasses of wine.

No, he decided, that didn't make sense. She appeared too capable in her work here. More than that, she clearly enjoyed it. This was no act.

Which raised even more doubts in his mind about

her brother's story. Where the hell was that report he'd requested?

But even without that report, he sensed there was something he was missing. What was the real reason for her running?

He watched her gather up plates from a table. Her blonde hair was tied back, but coiled tendrils had escaped to fall about her face as she dipped lower. He caught the moment she glanced over at him. She looked away and straightened the second she saw him watching her, before walking stiffly to the kitchen.

Oh yes, Princess, he thought, *I'm watching you.*

And maybe the only good thing was, it was no hardship to.

The night was growing old. The tables were thinning out, customers donning waterproof coats and jackets before exiting into the wild night air to board guest house buses or hire cars. Nobody was walking or had cycled tonight.

And the weather wasn't improving. From the few meteorological sites he'd been able to access during dinner, the cyclone was circling closer, the winds growing wilder. Some reports expected the winds to blow out overnight, while others expected conditions to persist for another day or two.

He didn't want to think about what that might mean. A twenty-four-hour delay had been bad enough.

The Princess appeared at his table to collect his empty plate. 'Would you like coffee or dessert, sir?'

'You don't have to act with me,' he said, tossing his napkin on the table. 'I'm not your target audience.'

She swiped her hands on her apron and smiled. 'I'm just doing my job.'

He didn't bother to smile back. 'And I'm just doing mine. As soon as this weather moves on, you're going home.'

Her smile brightened as if he hadn't just tried to puncture her mood. 'So, no coffee or dessert then?'

'No,' he growled, annoyed that she hadn't reacted. Okay, so she was probably feeling smug that the weather had delivered a twenty-four-hour delay in their departure, and by all accounts, there was a chance the same might happen again tomorrow, but he wanted her to show some vulnerability.

He wanted her to react. He wanted her to stop fighting the inevitable and accept that she was being taken home whether she liked it or not.

Damn it.

He wanted her to understand that he wasn't some plaything she could use to get her way. She needed to understand that he was no Luke or Mateo that she could use and bend to her will.

Instead, she was too confident. Too sure of herself for someone he'd taken to be young and innocent. Not that she'd turned out to be innocent given her experiences with the likes of Luke from Bondi and Mateo the barista, and certainly not after her late-night intrusion into his own bedroom last night. The Princess had been on the run for weeks. Goodness knows how many encounters she'd had along the way.

Was she imagining that he would be the next notch on her belt? Did she believe that if she managed to seduce him, that he'd change his mind about delivering her home?

Because if she thought that, then she wasn't just crazy. She was certifiable.

There was absolutely no chance of him getting involved with the Princess. She was his charge. His responsibility. Sure, she came all wrapped in a pretty package with her blonde hair and her sweet curves, but even if his body told him he was tempted—which he most certainly was not—she was forbidden to him.

Messing with the Princess would be a huge betrayal of professional trust. He wasn't about to sacrifice either his career or his business for this spoilt princess.

Whatever the Princess had in mind, whatever plan she had come up with to prevent her return to Rubanestein, it wasn't going to happen.

CHAPTER NINE

THE HEAD WAITER appeared in the centre of the restaurant, clapping his hands, getting the few remaining patrons' attention. 'Apologies, everyone, but I need to make an announcement. We've just been advised that the worst of the storm conditions will hit within the next two hours and may become quite dangerous. We want all of our guests and workers to get back to their accommodation safely before then. Consequently the restaurant will be closing a little early tonight. At this stage, if the forecast that the weather is easing during tomorrow is right, we expect to be open tomorrow for both lunch and dinner. Thank you for your patronage tonight. Get home safely and we'll see you next time.' He nodded and returned to his station by the door.

The restaurant rapidly emptied. The Princess appeared, clearing tables, collecting plates and cutlery. He left his seat and joined her, picking up plates from the rest of the tables.

'You're not expected to do that,' she said, frowning.

He shook his head. He wasn't doing it out of the kindness of his heart. He'd heard the tempest build outside. The Princess was his responsibility and all he wanted to do was ensure her safety. 'The sooner this place is cleaned up, the sooner we can get back to the apartment.' Their arms laden, they made their way to the kitchen, where Millie was busy loading the dishwasher. She looked up as they approached, her eyes widening as she saw Theo following Izzy.

He caught the Princess give Millie a brief shake of her head, as if to warn, *don't ask.*

Millie bit her lip, before smiling. 'Thanks, guys,' she said brightly, her voice at odds with the uncertain looks she sent from one to the other as they deposited their dishes on the sink. 'Appreciate it. You two better get away while you still can.'

It was a slow journey back to the apartment, the car crawling along the road in the wild weather, barely managing to achieve the speed limit, let alone exceed it. Even on the road bordering the protected lagoon, the seas were high, salt-laden spray and rain lashing the windscreen, the wipers battling to clear it before the next splatter. Winds buffeted the car, just like the palm trees either side of the road, the gusts pushing it sideways. Fronds torn from the palms crashed heavily onto the pavement around them.

It was wild.

Mad.

Scary.

The head waiter hadn't overstated the situation. If anything, the worst of the storm was impacting earlier. No wonder he'd wanted the patrons returned safely to their accommodations.

Izzy shivered as she looked out at the wild, untamed

night. Rain battered the roof of the car, so loud that it rendered speech impossible.

Until now, the island had provided her with sanctuary. Theo had threatened that when he'd found her, but Theo was not the least of her problems.

This storm was different. Instead of the island providing a sanctuary, for the first time Izzy felt threatened, not just for her future, but for her immediate safety. She could feel her fear in her shallow breathing and escalating heart rate as the storm raged around them—the howling winds, the raging lagoon to their right, the foliage whipping around the car in the wind.

Be careful what you wish for.

The cautionary tale was known worldwide, and it was true. Izzy had wished for their departure to be delayed and it had been, and now it looked very much like the airport wouldn't be reopening tomorrow, once again delaying Theo's attempts to return her to Rubanestein.

She'd got what she'd wished for.

But there was no victory. She felt no success. There was no easing to her nerves.

Nothing would ease her nerves while this storm raged around them.

Right now it was only Theo's driving expertise giving her a degree of comfort. She snatched her eyes off the road ahead to glance over at him, his gaze fixed on the road ahead while the threats kept coming from above and beside. He was frowning, she could tell in the soft light cast from the dashboard display, his jaw tense. Concentrating hard on keeping them safe.

She was grateful for his skill, as he negotiated a path around the debris on the road and out of the way that was being flung down from the treetops. So grateful that she wasn't driving. Even more grateful that she wasn't trying to make it back to the apartment on her bike.

Strange, she hadn't expected to feel grateful to Theo for anything. Theo was part of her problem. Escaping from him before he could take her back to her brother in Rubanestein was her mission. Maybe the storm and her nerves were getting to her.

Or maybe it was being trapped in a sedan with a man-mountain beside her. A warm man-mountain.

In the apartment she could get away from him. In the restaurant she'd been busy, too busy to spend time next to him. But trapped here in a small hire car, in the midst of a raging storm, he was too close, his masculine scent worming its way into her senses, the brush of his arm against hers as he changed gears in the small sedan ratcheting up the tension.

'The storm's getting worse,' she said, in a lull in the tattoo on the roof of the car. She could hear the tremor in her voice, the shakiness that spoke of her fear.

'Yes,' he simply answered, not averting his eyes as he concentrated fully on the road ahead. 'There's no way the airport will be reopening tomorrow. I expect you'll be happy about that.'

'Right now, I'll just be happy if you get us back safely. Tomorrow can take care of itself.'

There was no time to read his features, as another gust hit them, doing its best to blow the car off the road at the same time the beachside palms bent and thrashed under the onslaught.

Izzy saw it happen. Fast motion that seemed to happen in slow motion. A frond torn from on high that was

careening downwards, spinning, toppling directly towards their windscreen.

'Look out!' she cried, covering her eyes in case it
smashed into them.

Theo was already on it. He swerved wildly, pulling the
car away from the path of the toppling frond. Instead of
the windscreen, it slammed with a sickening thud onto
the hood and fender before crashing down onto the road.
The car bucked as the back tyre lurched over the thick
stem, before jolting back onto the road surface. Izzy let
go a breath she'd been holding.

'Are you all right?' he asked.

'I don't think I've ever been more scared in my life.'

'Hey,' he said, taking her hand in his, wrapping his
long fingers around hers and squeezing her hand reas-
suringly. 'I'm not going to let anything happen to you.'

*Because he was afraid he wouldn't get his reward
money?*

But the accusation she might once have immediately
launched at Theo refused to emerge from Izzy's mouth.
There was no way she would aggravate him while her
hand was encased in his, his hand lending her strength,
his strength feeding into hers.

Madness. Theo holding her hand. They didn't even
like each other. But that didn't mean she was about to
shrug his hand off hers. Not while her skin tingled at
his touch, and not just her hand itself, because warmth
seemed to radiate up her arm, filling her body with a
feeling unfamiliar to her. There was warmth there. There
was tenderness. But there was also a thirst, as if it didn't
have to end here.

He only let her hand go to change gears as he pulled into the driveway.

Izzy closed her eyes and leaned back into her seat. She'd never experienced near cyclonic conditions before. Everyone had told her that this brush would be mild. But if this was mild… And then there was Theo's generous gesture, to hold her hand and reassure her that all would be well.

And for the last few minutes of their journey, she'd felt completely safe.

He'd done that. Theo had made her feel safe.

Another deluge of rain unleashed on them.

'Okay?' he said.

She took a deep breath. 'Thank you for getting us back safely.'

He looked over at her then, a frown adding to a look of surprise on his face. A look of surprise that evaporated a moment after she'd witnessed it, so much that she wondered whether she'd imagined it.

'We got here,' he said. 'Are you ready to make a run for it.'

Izzy looked at the rain pounding the car. 'You don't have an umbrella?'

'An umbrella would be next to useless in these conditions. Stay there.' He pushed open his door and rounded the car to her door. He pulled her door open, threw his jacket over her head and shoulders as she emerged from the car, and with his arm around her, set off to race the few metres through the pelting rain to the door.

Everything happened so quickly. They were racing for the front door, getting battered by the heavy wind and rain, when Izzy's foot slipped on the wet surface.

She stumbled, only for Theo to catch her, tumbling her into his arms to carry her to the sheltered space by the front door.

A moment later, they were inside, the door slammed behind them against the weather, both of them panting hard as Theo leaned with her against the wall. He let go her legs, letting her find her feet, but he kept hold, his free hand going to her waist, as if to make sure she wouldn't collapse to the floor.

She was still catching her breath after their frantic dash to the door, her arms still wrapped around Theo's neck, when a bubble of laughter escaped Izzy's mouth. At the madness of their desperate dash. At relief at being inside and out of the immediate danger of the storm.

'Wow,' she said, sounding as breathless as she felt, 'you are quite the hero. Driving safely through the storm. Getting us both unscathed to the front door. Thank you.'

Her mistake was turning her face up to his. She'd expected to see her laughter mirrored in his eyes. She'd expected their relief at escaping the storm to be shared.

Instead, when she looked into his features and into his dark, dark eyes staring into hers, she saw no humour. Instead, she saw need. She saw—*hunger.*

And she knew he wasn't still holding her because he was worried she'd topple to the floor. He was holding her because he didn't want to let go.

Her heart lurched. Her breath hitched. She licked her lips.

His eyes dipped, following the movement of her tongue. Time stretched as if made of wire, pulled taut by conflicting forces. Slow motion became slower. How was that even possible, when your blood throbbed faster, harder, your ears ringing with the sound of the blood pumping around your body, blocking out the sound of the rain pelting down outside.

Theo looked down at her, his dark eyes tortured and wild like the tempest outside. He muttered two strained words. 'Princess,' he said gruffly. 'Isabella.'

His lips brushed hers in a pass as tender as a butterfly's kiss yet still enough to make her entire body tremble. Her back arched, her arms winding more tightly around his neck, her lips melding with his, welcoming the contact. Parting softly when he ran his tongue along the line of her mouth. As if tasting her. Inviting his kiss.

Her tremor seemed to trigger something inside him. He made a sound, a low groan that came from the back of his throat, a groan that spoke of uncoiling need, of letting go. Then his arms suddenly tightened around her, collecting her closer as he deepened the kiss.

And like the storm raging around them, his kiss stormed her senses, sending her thoughts into turmoil, challenging everything she thought she knew about this man. Challenging everything she thought she knew about kissing. His lips were warm and yet surprisingly soft, his mouth was hot, his tongue knew how to do things she'd never imagined. Her senses were full of him, his taste, his heated touch, his breath mingling with hers, his own masculine scent, musky and warm. It was an onslaught to both her body and her senses. Every part of her—every cell it seemed—was attuned to him. Preparing for him. Nipples straining. Her thighs thrumming. It was almost too much but at the same time, she never wanted it to end.

And it was like everything she'd planned. Only better.

Seducing the bodyguard.

This is what she had wanted. This is what she had planned, hoping to bend Theo to her will.

But planning and execution were two different things.

Execution was threatening to make her forget what her plan actually was…

Right now she didn't care about her plan. All she cared about was the feel of Theo hard up against her, his mouth on hers, his big hands spanning her waist, his long fingers achingly close to the breasts that hungered for his touch, her nipples jutting hard and straining against his chest, the humming between her thighs becoming a symphony.

And she wanted more.

'Theo,' she whispered breathlessly between kisses, her hands framing his whiskered face. The man was a masterclass in contrasting textures. Soft yet firm lips, a whiskered jaw, the hard wall of his chest and abs and the heat of his hands. So much to explore. So much to discover.

If he'd heard her utter his name, he made no acknowledgement. He was under the same magical spell that she was, the outside storm moved inside.

His mouth moved back to hers, his lips meshing with hers, his tongue dancing with hers, and Izzy lost the will to think and gave herself up to sensation.

The sound of his name came as a vague intrusion on his thoughts. But only vague. He had more important things to consider. Like the woman he held in his arms. Her taste was like a drug and now he was addicted. An addict that wanted a fix.

An addict who was seriously in need of a fix.

And he intended to get it.

The crash outside tugged at his senses, senses that were fully diverted elsewhere. But the sound was as unsettling as it was unwelcome. The sound said something was wrong, and no mere desire to ignore it—not even this woman melting into his arms and body—could make it go away.

With an iron will he put his hands on her shoulders, stood back, and took a deep breath.

She stood in front of him, her hazel eyes looking dazed and confused, her pink lips plumped and parted. And with the force of a sledgehammer, it hit him. He'd been kissing the Princess—the woman he was engaged to protect—the woman he'd wanted to make love to.

And red-hot anger—at her for being who she was—but mostly at himself, for forgetting who she was—surged through his veins.

What the hell had he been thinking? He dropped his hands from her shoulders and turned away. That was an easy question to answer. He hadn't been thinking. Not with his brain.

Instead, she'd looked up at him with those innocent hazel eyes, uttering her words of thanks from that lush mouth, and relief that they'd escaped the storm had only served to ignite yet another storm. A storm that had been brewing ever since he'd laid eyes on the Princess. A storm between the two of them.

Gamo!

She was a princess.

She was his responsibility.

He had no place kissing her.

He spun back. She was still looking confused. 'What's

wrong,' she said, looking like she was about to slide down the wall behind her. Which only served to remind him of how liquid she'd felt in his arms.

Vlaka!

What wasn't wrong? He hit his forehead with the heel of his hand. He was a fool. But there was no time for that now. 'Didn't you hear it?'

'Hear what?'

'The crash.'

She shook her head, still looking confused. 'What crash?'

He ran his hand through his hair. Pulled open the door and stepped outside into the storm. Where the cause of the crash became obvious. A tall palm tree from the beach had been toppled, blocking the road, its crown landing mere inches from the front door, its remaining fronds splayed and distorted haplessly against the ground.

Thankfully no damage done. Not to the outside of the property. As far as Theo was concerned, the damage had all been wreaked inside. No, it had started before that, when he'd taken her hand in the car to reassure her. She'd been so afraid. She'd felt so fragile. He'd wanted to reassure her. But he'd felt her hand tremble in his and he wanted to protect her. He was a bodyguard, that was what he did. Protect people. Rescue people.

He hadn't expected to enjoy it so much.

He hadn't expected to wish their journey might be longer.

Gamo! He was a fool.

He phoned Tom Parker while he was outside, to let him know that a palm had fallen and that the road was blocked. In reality, it gave him a further excuse not to go back inside yet, something he didn't want to do until he got his thoughts and his wayward body in order. He needed to stand outside in the blustery winds and lashing rain until the last vestiges of desire-fuelled body heat had been exorcised from his flesh.

He'd kissed the Princess. And not just a passing kiss. He'd made it obvious he'd like to take it further. God, his hands had been all over her, he would have taken it further if a falling palm tree hadn't intervened. It didn't matter that she hadn't tried to stop him. He didn't trust her as far as he could throw her, not after her first night's expedition. After that, he didn't trust her that she might employ her newly found wiles to make him complicit in her attempts to avoid a return to Rubanestein.

Phone call made, Theo took another deep breath, turned, and went inside.

The Princess was nowhere to be seen. He towelled off the worst of the rain, and heard a sound from the kitchen, like mugs landing on a counter. He stopped as she came into sight. She was making coffee, putting a capsule into a machine. She looked over at him, her eyes bright but suspicious. 'Everything all right?'

'A palm tree has fallen across the road. Thankfully no other damage.'

She smiled. 'I wasn't talking about that.'

'Princess,' he said, hauling in a deep breath as the fingers of one hand raked through his hair. 'I'm sorry.'

She frowned. 'What for?'

'For kissing you. I shouldn't have done that. I overstepped the mark. Please forgive me.'

'You didn't enjoy it? I got the impression—'

He snarled. 'It's not about enjoyment. You are my charge. My responsibility.'

'So you did enjoy it?'

'I didn't say that.'

'You didn't not say it either.'

'Stop it,' he said, his fingers now stroking his brow. 'Bottom line, it was a mistake, Princess. It should never have happened. I promise it won't happen again.'

'But how can I be sure it won't?' she said.

'What?'

'I've heard of this before. You seem to assume that I kissed you because I wanted to. But it's a known phenomenon. It's called Stockholm Syndrome, where a captive finds herself enamoured of her captor.'

'I am not your captor.'

'It feels like it. And here we are. Forced together in close proximity.'

'Not my choice. You would already be home if a cyclone hadn't intervened.'

'So now we're forced to weather out the storm together. Is it any wonder that you might become the focus of my attentions?'

'Don't do that,' he said gruffly.

'Don't do what?'

'Try to convince me that something is happening when it's not. Try to make it look like you are attracted to me, whatever your reason, when all you want to do is escape from me.'

'Why can't the two coexist together? Do I have to hate you to want to not be returned to Rubanestein? Why can't I appreciate how sexy you are while still not wanting to be forced back to the hell-hole of what will be my future existence?'

He shook his head, trying to shake away her compliment. He would not be touched by her empty compliments. 'No. Not happening. And you're getting a bit melodramatic again, Princess.'

'Am I? Then how about we put the boot on the other foot, as unlikely as it might be. What if you'd been promised in marriage to a fifty-something-year-old woman against your will, when you'd been always told by your father that you could marry for love, and no matter how far you ran, someone would search the world to drag you back to comply with someone else's wishes? How would you feel?'

He stood stock-still. 'You're saying this man your evil brother has promised you to is in his fifties?'

'Yes, he's in his fifties. But why should age even come into it? Whatever the age, how is it possible that you could wilfully return me to this hell, and to marrying a man that I have been sold to, a man that I can never love? A man that I will never love, knowing the circumstances of our union.'

Her words were tumbling over each other, her colour was high, her eyes beseeching him to believe her.

Theo had to hand it to her. If she were acting, she was giving one hell of a good performance. Theo knew that the Princess would stop at nothing to prevent her return to Rubanestein, and she'd now supplemented the forced marriage story by adding the age detail, in case he wasn't already sympathetic. The Princess was twenty-five years old, and to be promised—if that's what was happening— to someone, a colleague of her brother and not a partner she'd chosen to spend the rest of her life with—that was wrong. And yet, she wasn't a teenager, she was an adult, which raised even more questions.

'When did you think you were going to get married?'

'What?'

'You're twenty-five, and I'm guessing, you have no boyfriend waiting in the wings for your return.'

'And your point is?'

'My point is, it occurs to me that if you'd already been married, your brother—if I am to believe your story— wouldn't be able to marry you off so readily.'

She looked up at him with incredulous eyes. 'You're blaming me not being married for my brother's actions? Are you serious?'

'You have to admit, if you were already married, you wouldn't have a problem. You wouldn't have had to flee.'

'I don't believe it. You are blaming me.'

'No, I'm just saying… No, I'm asking. I'm sorry, Princess, because it's not like you're unattractive, and yet there's been nobody you've been interested in? Nobody you wanted to spend the rest of your life with?' He'd met Sophia in university, and what started as a friendship had soon turned to love. 'I'm having trouble understanding that.'

She blinked. Long slow blinks that told him she had little regard for his words. 'Thank you, I think. But for the record, there has been plenty of interest—in me. Apparently being a member of the royal family—a "not unattractive" princess with ready access to palaces and riches attracts plenty of interest. My problem has been determining who is more interested in me, for who I am, rather than my place in the monarchy.' She cocked one side of her mouth. 'As you admitted, you wouldn't understand.'

Ouch.

Theo deserved that. The Princess was wiser and more grounded than he'd ever anticipated. He bowed his head. 'Once again, Princess, I need to apologise.'

'Accepted,' she said brusquely. 'And now, I think I'll turn in. Sleep well.'

She breezed past him and headed up the stairs. He listened to her footfall, heard the slow click of her door closing, and knew there was no sleep waiting for him. Whatever point he'd been trying to make, he'd badly botched. Although it did help him understand why someone as attractive as the Princess hadn't been snatched up already. *Theos.* He'd called her "not unattractive".

It was a wonder she hadn't slapped him across the face.

He glanced at his watch. The Princess was right, it was time to turn in. Time to be done with watching her. Time to be out of her presence. He'd told himself he wasn't attracted to her. He'd tried to convince herself of that. He couldn't afford to be attracted to her.

But truth was, he needed to get away from her, to get out of her presence, before he started to believe her story.

The night was one howling mess. The wind blew, the rain lashed, and the palm tree fronds rattled as they shook and smacked into each other. Theo barely slept, wishing the storm would die down so that the airport would open, no matter how unlikely that seemed with the racket going on outside, and that they could fly out tomorrow. Hoping that he wouldn't be hijacked during the night again. He'd employed the same improvised alarms that he'd employed the night before, his bedroom door was still open in case the Princess tried to flee out the front door, but tonight he'd secured his door with a tie to ensure it couldn't be pushed open enough to allow someone access—if he even managed to snatch a moment of sleep.

He needed desperately to sleep, but it was too dangerous. He turned over in his bed, punching his pillow into submission.

Given what had happened earlier this evening, if the Princess did find a way into his room again, knowing what he knew and how good she felt, would he even bother to send her away?

Of course, he would.

It was ridiculous even contemplating the question. But the fact he'd even had to ask himself required some serious analysis.

Never before had he felt the pull of attraction for one of his rescues. And not since Sophia had he felt the power of attraction for any woman. No woman could take the place of Sophia. So why did the Princess affect him so?

She was both a rescue and a Princess. Double the reason to deliver her safely home untouched by him. He had a contract to find and return her.

He had a duty to return her.

Attraction didn't come into it.

Her story about her brother selling her off didn't come into it. That wasn't part of his remit. That wasn't something he was contracted to consider. His job was to get her home. End of story.

Except...

Her story still niggled at his conscience. The idea that

she'd run away because the Prince planned to marry off his sister in order to settle his gambling debts was fanciful. A fancy she'd then embellished by saying the man she'd been promised to was in his fifties.

Trying to convince him by enhancing the injustice? An attempt to further appeal to his sense of right and wrong by stressing their difference in ages? She'd got him there. The idea that he was returning her home only to be forced to marry a man in his fifties that she wanted no part of—that wouldn't just be a waste.

It would be a crime.

The Princess was young and vibrant and was entitled to be living her life with the man of her choice.

But if she were lying and her story completely fabricated?

On the other hand, her brother's story was equally thin. The Princess didn't look in the least bit worried or envious about not being the one to occupy Rubanestein's throne. If the Princess was so certain she should be the one to sit on the throne, surely she would be bagging her brother's efforts at ruling the principality, pulling him down at every opportunity, pushing her own credibility to perform the role instead. On the contrary, she seemed more interested in just being able to live her life the way she wanted.

Certainly, she'd run for a reason. But right now, uncomfortably, her story was making the more sense.

So where did that leave him? She didn't mean anything to him, not really, other than providing endless irritation one way or another. When she wasn't needling him with her smart tongue, she was driving him to distraction with her lush mouth or her beguiling eyes or her all too bewitching body. She was a pint-sized distraction he didn't need. It would be a relief to see the back of her.

And given he was contracted to return her to Rubanestein, what choice did he have?

CHAPTER TEN

THEO WAS UP before dawn because lying in bed and not sleeping was getting old. A crew came out at first light to clear the road of the fallen palm, Tom delivering the news that the airport would remain closed another day.

It didn't matter that Theo had been half expecting it, given the weather, but the complications of this case were grating on his nerves. Never before had he felt so many conflicting emotions in carrying out a recovery, none of them wanting to be resolved any time soon.

The storm was no longer above and around him. The storm was in his head. A royal storm, named Isabella, occupying his headspace, blotting out reason, testing his patience along with his willpower.

He should never have kissed her. That one thought had played on a loop through his head throughout the night. He should never have touched the Princess. There was no greater truth.

The woman was trouble. She threatened his equilibrium at every turn. She tested his resolve. Worst of all, holding her had felt like someone had turned on a light in his life. Kissing her had felt like hope.

It was so long since he'd felt hope.

* * *

So merely telling himself again and again that he
shouldn't have kissed her—*knowing it*—didn't make it
any easier to accept it. Didn't make it any easier to re-
gret it.

The woman was trouble all right.

No wonder she was messing with his head.

He was sitting at the dining room table on his second pot
of coffee when the Princess appeared in the kitchen looking bright-eyed and well-rested. He sighed. Of course
she was.

'Sleep well?' she asked, helping herself to a cup.

It was all he could do not to growl. And not just at the
sight of her in her robe, untied of course, and no doubt
designed to show off her shortie pyjamas and her perfect legs. What she lacked in height, she made up for in
shapeliness, all sweet curves and toned flesh. He turned
his eyes away. 'I suspect you know the answer to that.'

'Shame,' she said, covering her mouth with her free
hand on a yawn. 'I slept really well.' She moved to the
window and stood staring out at the view a while. 'Wow,
I can see the tops of Mt Gower and Lidgbird. The weather
seems to be clearing.'

'Just not enough.'

'Oh,' she said, taking a sip of her coffee. 'Bad news for
you, then. Although I have to confess not being sorry.'

He grunted. 'I didn't think so.'

'So,' she said turning back, 'what are we going to do
today?'

'Why do we have to "do" anything?'

'Because we can't spend the entire day inside.'

'I'm perfectly happy spending the day inside.'

'Okay, so there's always the pool, I guess. I could soak in there a while.'

He squeezed his eyes shut. Not the pool. Not the strapless bikini with that little ruffle at the top. Please god, not the tiny bikini again. He was supposed to be reminding himself of all the reasons he needed not to touch her. He was supposed to be keeping his distance. He didn't need a refresher of those sweet curves. But how attractive could the plunge pool actually be after the storm? 'I'm sure the pool will be uninviting—it no doubt needs cleaning after all the debris from the storm landing in it.'

'Hmm.' She seemed to weigh that up as she looked out the window to the deck and the pool outside. 'There is a lot of rubbish in it.'

'There you go,' he said, wanting to sigh in relief.

She turned and pulled out a chair opposite his at the table. 'In that case, I guess we'll just have to chat.'

He pinched the bridge of his nose between thumb and forefinger. 'Or you could get dressed.'

'I will. After breakfast.' She looked around. 'What is for breakfast by the way?'

'I don't know. The maid must be taking a day off. Why don't you look in the pantry and fridge to see what there is to eat?'

'Wow. Somebody got out of bed on the wrong side this morning. Or have you just been taking cranky pills again?'

The smile she added at the end of the sentence was the kicker.

His chair scraped on the floor as he pushed it back, rising to his feet to put more than a table's width between them. 'I'm not cranky,' he said, his turn to look out the windows to the incredible mountain vista that lay beyond. Okay, so it was a lie, but what did she expect, making out that everything was sweetness and light between them when she knew—she damned well knew—that she was goading him, torturing him, with her every appearance, her every word.

She must know that kiss last night was a mistake. She must know the danger she was putting him in—acting in his own interests instead of his client's, and messing with a rescue, a princess no less. He had no place. He had no right.

And yet she seemed so carefree. Almost as if she took delight from tempting him. Had her conquests in Sydney given her confidence and licence to explore her new-found skills while she still had some say?

He was sure her time back in the palace in Rubanestein would be more regulated, controlled. Even if she tried, she would be known and recognised by the populace. There would be no more casual encounters with someone at the beach or in a café somewhere.

Was this her final fling?

Did she have him lined up as her final fling?

If that's what she'd planned, she was way out of luck, because there was no way he was falling for that. No way he'd give in to her. Sure, she'd felt like light and hope in his arms, but that was an illusion. Something she'd wanted him to feel. Because there could be no light. There was no hope.

Not after Sophia.

Not with anyone.

Especially not with Princess Isabella.

* * *

The beguiling scent broke him out of his thoughts. Of onions browning, of capsicum, tomatoes, mushrooms and more. A toaster pinged. He turned to see her adding scrambled eggs to a skillet filled with sauteed vegetables.

She saw him looking at her. 'Hungry?' she asked as she added grated parmesan to the mix.

His stomach growled. Coffee could only go so far. 'You cook?' he asked.

'Of course, I cook. I'm a multitasking princess. Is the concept unfamiliar to you?'

It was out of context. Nothing in the information he'd been provided had pointed to her having a fondness for cooking. It made no sense. When given a dossier on a rescue, everything on the rescue was disclosed. Every like and dislike was listed. Everything that could give insight into where a recovery expert could trace them. Everything.

Who had prepared this dossier? Someone working for her brother? Someone who didn't know her?

'You're frowning,' she said, as she served up three-quarters of the skillet onto a plate for him.

His eyebrows shot north. 'I'm still getting used to the fact you can cook.'

She smiled. 'My father taught me.'

'The Prince?'

'He loved being in the kitchen with my mother. After her influence, he told me that if he hadn't been born a Prince, he would happily have become a chef. Simple food mostly, but good food.' She pointed to his food. 'Sit down. Try it.'

Theo duly sat. Picked up his fork. Sampled a mouth-

ful. And was blown away by the simple yet perfect
combination of the ingredients. 'To think I wasted your
talents yesterday by serving you a piece of toast.'

Her smile permeated all the way into his bones. 'Don't
beat yourself up. It was good toast.'

And even his bones felt happy until he thought about
what she was doing. Why was she trying to please him?
What was her angle? He couldn't afford to let down his
guard now. Tomorrow by all accounts they would fly out
of Lord Howe Island. A scant two hours later they would
be back in his jet en route to Rubanestein.

He had to keep his guard up. He wasn't about to be
waylaid now, not so close to closing this deal.

The frittata was delicious. Another cup of coffee
washed it down. Theo was feeling fully satisfied and
replete.

And the best thing? The Princess had gone upstairs
to shower and change after breakfast.

One more day, he told himself. Twenty-four hours.
He'd suffered through worse. The airport was expected
to open tomorrow and he'd pulled strings to make sure
they were on the first plane out. The end was in sight.

And once he'd delivered her home, he might even be
able to forget about this woman's beguiling accent and
her fresh citrusy scent and the too-sweet curves of her
body. He might even be able to stop thinking about her
twenty-four hours of the day.

He could hardly wait.

Isabella looked at her scant wardrobe. She'd brought only
basic items with her to Lord Howe Island. Beachwear.

Casual clothes. Sundresses. Along with shorts and jeans and T-shirts to get her through any days of work.

She surveyed her meagre collection, wanting something that Theo hadn't seen. That might just tip him over the edge. He was close. She hadn't had much experience with men, but she could see that he was battling his own inner demons. Trying to pretend she didn't affect him when she was clearly driving him crazy. Otherwise, why would he be so awkward around her?

A jumpsuit caught her attention. A jumpsuit she'd found at a Saturday market on the Sydney coast that spoke of summer and would be a forever reminder of her time down under. Cap-sleeved and short legged with a printed fruit salad pattern, watermelon, pineapple, dragon fruit on a white woven cotton background. Now that the weather had moderated, she knew it was the perfect choice for the day ahead.

Theo was drinking yet another cup of coffee when she reappeared downstairs.

He looked up. Took her in. Immediately looked down again.

'You probably shouldn't drink so much coffee,' she said.

'Thanks for the advice,' he said. 'Next time, wait until I ask for it.'

She snorted. 'I did tell you, you've been taking cranky pills.'

'I'm not cranky.'

'So you say, and yet, you seem so defensive.'

Defence was the best form of offence. But he didn't have to react to her ridiculous claims. He didn't have to prove anything.

She sat down opposite him, her jumpsuit at least hiding more of her than her pyjamas had done.

'So if we're not going out, maybe we could use this opportunity to learn more about each other.'

'Like what?'

'You were married, right?'

'Yes.'

'And you loved her?'

'Of course I did.'

'And she loved you.'

'Princess,' he said, his voice thick. 'Where is this going?'

'But she did, right?'

The words felt like they'd been wrenched from his soul. 'She did.' Not that he'd been able to honour that love, not in the end.

She seemed to contemplate that for a minute. 'What did that feel like—to have someone love you so much?'

'It was—perfection.'

'I love that,' she said. 'That is everything every person wants.'

And Theo knew exactly where this was going before she'd even uttered her next words.

'Because that's what I want. To feel someone to love me so much and me love him that it's perfection.'

'It's a worthy goal,' he said, intentionally keeping his distance.

'My father promised that I could marry for love. I was never going to accede to the throne, so he promised me that I could make my own way. But how am I to find that love, how am I ever to feel that same feeling, if my brother is to marry me off to someone I don't love. Someone I could never love?'

Her voice was rising. 'Princess—again, you're becoming over melodramatic.'

'You don't believe me,' she said. 'You don't believe what my brother has in store for me.'

'There are no indications.' He'd had nothing back on his request for information but given the threadbare Wi-Fi and the weather, that was hardly surprising. Then again, maybe it was because there was nothing to find.

'No indications? What are you waiting for? Of course he's not going to "give you indications". He needs you onside. He needs you to deliver the goods. And that's all I am to him. The goods. The ticket out of his massive debts.'

He said nothing. Given the lack of any evidence, there was nothing to say. She sipped her coffee and he assumed she was done.

He was wrong.

'My brother has always had a mean streak,' she said, flopping into a chair, rubbing her forehead with one hand. 'It was always tempered when my parents were alive, but even when they weren't around he'd find ways to bully me. I thought once he acceded to the throne, he'd have enough on his plate to worry about and he'd forget about me. But I was wrong.'

Theo looked up. A bully? There had been something in the dossier that had hinted at the Prince's authoritarian personality, and his strong need to control, but this had been painted as unsurprising, given his station and the leadership role expected of him. But could there be something darker behind it?

'Did he ever hurt you? Physically, I mean.'

She sniffed. 'No. Not me. Nothing that would show. But I had a six-month-old puppy called Coco. My parents had given her to me for my twelfth birthday.'

Chills skittered down Theo's spine. 'What happened?'

'I couldn't find her one day. I called and called but she didn't come. And then Rafael appeared, holding Coco. It was wrong. Coco hated Rafael, she growled whenever he was around. But now she was crying. Whimpering. And I could see that one of her legs was just hanging. Limp. She fell down the stairs, Rafael told me, and then he smiled. And I knew—I just knew that he'd done it. My parents believed him—maybe they just wanted to believe him—because my father visited me that night while Coco was being cared for in the veterinary hospital. He hugged me tightly and told me that he was sorry for how the way things were. He told me that things would be different one day. He promised me—' She pulled her legs up onto the chair and wrapped her arms tightly around them.

And Theo's senses were stretched piano-wire tight. He ached to get up and wrap his arms around her and comfort her—but that was because it provided him with the perfect excuse to do so. To do exactly what he wanted to do. But he couldn't reach out. He couldn't afford to make a move.

Her story might be compelling. Heart-rending, even. But convincing? And did it even matter? She was a rescue. He was a bodyguard. She was his mission. No matter what he felt right now, emotions didn't come into it. His job was to get her home, no matter the sob stories along the way.

No matter how hard it might feel.

* * *

Nothing was working. Izzy rose from her chair to pace the suite. She didn't know how to break through the walls that Theo had erected around him, walls that seemed to offer a crack, a crevice, a mere promise every now and then to let her in to get a glimpse of the man and let him see her, only to have him plaster over those walls, raise the drawbridge and withdraw into the inner sanctum.

One night. One more night was all she had to convince him not to take her home. She took a deep breath as she looked out the window at the grey skies, the swirling clouds around the tops of the mountains and the swaying palm trees of the rainforest below.

But she wasn't done with trying yet. Maybe she just needed to try a different tack…

'So,' she said, turning, 'you were married.'

He looked up from the messages he was reading on his phone that the trickle of internet had finally allowed through. There was a crisis developing in a recovery happening in Istanbul, a complication with another in Athens, and he was still waiting on information he'd urgently requested about Prince Rafael, but his attention was now one hundred per cent focused on the question this woman had just asked.

Where the hell had that come from? Unless this was another tilt at the fifty-year-old fiancé thing. He half expected her next question to be, *'How old was she?'*

'I think we've established that I was married, Princess.'

'And you've made love with a woman.'

'What's that got to do with anything?'

'You're right. Silly question. You were married and of course you would have made love with your wife, and probably a bunch of women besides.'

'Not while I was married to my wife.' *Not since, for that matter.* 'Now where is this going, Princess?'

She shrugged. 'Only that you're a man. And you look like someone who would know how all the bits might work.'

There was no preventing his eyebrows shooting north. 'I doubt there are many adults alive on this planet who don't know how "all the bits might work". I'm equally sure your education, not to mention your recent experiences, will have filled you in on the necessary details.'

'Well, of course it did, I just wondered what it felt like from the male point of view.'

'Didn't Mateo or Luke or whoever else there was bother to share that information with you?'

Isabella's interest spiked. Theo remembered their names? That *was* interesting.

She shrugged. 'I guess I was too caught up in the moment. I didn't think to ask. So now I'm asking you.'

He bristled on his chair. 'I wish you wouldn't. I'm not comfortable talking about this with you, Princess. It's not appropriate.'

'Not even in general? I'm not asking for specifics. I'm not asking for a blow-by-blow analysis.'

He shook his head. 'Believe me, that's the last thing you're going to get.'

'Right. So, what can you tell me?'

'Nothing,' he said. He slammed his laptop shut.

Twenty-four hours had never seemed so long. 'I can't stand another moment of this.'

'So, you agree, we're going out?'

It wasn't his first choice. His first choice would be to lock her in her room where she couldn't constantly needle him with her perfect body and her smart words. But locking her in her room, even if it was possible, was crossing a line he'd never expected to want to cross.

What was it with this woman?

'Well?' she said, looking decidedly more sheepish but not giving up, her hands clasped innocently before her. 'It has to be better than staying here with you getting on my nerves and me getting on yours.'

It was ridiculous. Going out in this wild weather was ridiculous. But maybe she had a point. Staying here with this woman in this apartment for however long the storm was going to last was impossible. He might not be attracted to her—he refused to admit the truth that he was attracted to her—but just being in her proximity was on his mind—and her nerves—one hundred per cent of the time.

'What did you have in mind?'

Ten minutes later they pulled up at the island's visitor centre. The rain had eased although the winds were still high, the palm fronds thrashing above their heads. 'So why are we here?' Theo asked.

'To learn,' she said, 'it's interesting.'

Theo doubted it, but what else did he have to do? And maybe it would give him a break from the constant headache that was trying to exist in close proximity to this woman.

Inside there was a café and store that sold books and all manner of souvenirs. A family sat at a table in the café, eating lunch.

Theo wasn't a tourist. Souvenirs didn't interest him. But he stopped to pick up the odd book and flick through the pages. He looked up and realised he'd lost sight of the Princess. His heart missed a beat. Had the Princess sneaked out the door while he was reading? Had she used this excursion as cover for one more of her attempts to escape? But no—he caught a glance of her through a doorway leading to another room. He put the book down and headed in. It was clearly the museum part of the building, overflowing with naval and aerial artefacts along with evidence and artefacts from the island's whaling past. The history of the island was laid bare in the displays. The island might be tiny, but it had a big history. Formed from the remnants of an ancient volcanic eruption, there were black and white pictures of times gone by where there had been no airport or runway and when seaplanes had serviced the island, taking off and landing on the lagoon. And then there was a case containing bones, a skeleton of something resembling a massive turtle, at least a metre long, but this turtle came with a skull bedecked in a tiara of horns and a permanent grimace. The bones of its long tail were similarly barbed. It looked menacing and fierce.

'It looks grumpy, doesn't it?' she said, appearing next to him unexpectedly, bringing with her the fresh citrus scent she wore. He edged away. Once he'd realised she hadn't tried to run away, he'd been enjoying another brief moment of space away from her, but that opportunity had clearly come to an end. He didn't want her so close to him. The whole purpose of the outing was about getting some distance from each other, but here she was, edging up next to him and setting the nerve endings in his skin on red alert. Hadn't she told him that he was getting on her nerves? She was showing no signs of it. Instead, she seemed intent on crowding his space. What was her game?

His senses bristled at the proximity. He was hoping that he could make it through the day unscathed, without another attempt by her to seduce him, without another stupid kiss he'd planted on her.

Unscathed?

Theo wondered if it were possible. The longer he spent in this woman's presence, the more he felt scathed—by her mere presence, by her touch.

By her scent, fresh and citrusy, that suited her perfectly.

By her lips. Enticing. Full and pink.

By her eyes. Her impossible cat-like eyes. Hazel. Or were they more amber, with flecks of gold in their depths? Eye colour that seemed to change with the light.

'I told you it was interesting, didn't I?'

She had and as much as he hadn't cared one way or another, the small museum was full of surprising displays and facts. The tiny dot of an island in the middle of the Tasman Sea, halfway between Australia and New Zealand, had a rich and fascinating history.

'It's an ancient horned turtle,' she said, not waiting for him to answer. 'They used to live on the island around forty thousand years ago.'

He nodded. 'I think I'm relieved they don't still live here.'

She laughed. 'Wow, you made a joke. How about that?'

Had he? He'd thought he was merely stating a fact.

'You know what, though?' she said, looking from the skeleton to Theo and back. 'There's a definite resemblance. It reminds me of you.'

He snorted. 'Very funny.'

'No, seriously. He looks cranky and fierce. Just like you.'

Excellent. She was comparing him to a forty-thousand-year-old skeleton. He turned away, as much to escape a scent that was becoming more alluring by the minute, as to get out of range of her verbal barbs. There was a reason for his crankiness, and the Princess was a big part of it.

Wrong, he corrected himself a moment later. The Princess *was* the reason for it.

'Are we done here?' he asked, impatient to move on in case she started comparing him to more of the relics in the museum.

'If you're ready.'

Theo was more than ready.

The Princess directed him up a hill and along a ridge that seemed to run along the spine of the island, before taking a right turn that led them down a beach. It was a small bay on the northern side of the island, with a cluster of rocky islands out to sea and with grassy picnic grounds adjoining the sandy beach, where wave tumbled over wave on their frenetic way to the shore. Nobody was picnicking today. Theirs was the only car in the car park. Clearly, they were the only mad people who wanted to be out in this weather. Everyone else must be hunkered down riding out the storm.

'Okay,' he said, thinking they were on a fool's errand. Getting out of the apartment to avoid getting on each other's nerves might have sounded like a good plan, but it wasn't like they weren't together. As far as he could tell, it didn't matter where they were—they were still going to get on each other's nerves. 'So, we're here. Why?'

She smiled on a shrug and once again he was struck by the change in his perception of her, that once he'd thought she looked like a teenager with all those mad colours in her hair, young and innocent. She wasn't an innocent—he knew that now—and maybe that's why she looked like a woman. And yet still her delight right now was more like that teenager, or maybe, he conceded, someone who had discovered something special. Was it really that special? 'Come and see,' she said.

The wind caught her door, flinging it open. She whooped as she grabbed at it, fighting against the wind to close it.

He sighed. Utter madness. He followed her out onto a path leading to the beach. The wind whipped at his hair, tugging at his shirt. She stopped at a shelter containing a basic vending machine.

'What is that?' he asked, as she exchanged coins for two bags.

'You'll see,' she said. He didn't see anything beyond the loosened tendrils of her hair whipping around her face in the wind. 'I'll show you.'

She led him down towards the water, kicked off her sandals on the sand, and waded into the water. She looked back at him, while he was still wondering what the point of this was. The wind was still wild, clouds building, whitecaps mashing on the sea. The sea was a mess. It would rain later, the forecast predicted. 'What are you waiting for?' she yelled over her shoulder. He could barely hear her over the gusting wind. He was still waiting to discover the point of this mad venture.

She threw out one arm and whooped, or was it a scream? Suddenly, the water around her bare legs frothed and churned and it looked like whatever it was under those turbulent waves was trying to eat the Princess alive.

Did they even have piranha in Australia? Or was it one of those ancient horned turtles that hadn't died out after all?

'Princess!' he called, tossing off his shoes and ploughing into the water, determined to get to her. He hadn't put up with all he had to lose her now. He reached her and swooped her into his arms, but something was missing. *Blood.* There was no blood. Surely if she was being attacked, there would be blood.

And surely, he'd be being attacked right now too. And while something down there bumped and nudged his legs, there was a remarkable absence of teeth.

'What are you doing?' she laughed, grinning madly in his arms.

Good question. What was he doing?

'Put me down,' she said, laughing. 'The fish are missing the tourists.'

Fish?

And the nudging and bumping into his calves suddenly made sense. He put her down and she handed him a small bag. 'Here, take this.' He looked at it. Tried to make sense of the label. Fish food. That's why they were standing in the shallows while the tail end of a cyclone whipped the air around them? They were here to feed fish? She had to be kidding.

But he could feel the slap of warm bodies against his ankles and shins before he could discern them in the choppy water. 'You see,' she said, laughing as she scattered around some of the fish food. 'Look!'

The water whirled and swirled around his knees, whipped up by the wind, but yes, he could make out the fish crowding around his legs. Big fish, small fish, some silvery and sleek, some long and fluid, some brightly coloured, more fish than he'd ever seen in one place in the wild, but all of them angling for a treat. And with every wave breaking on the shore, it brought still more fish.

'So feed them,' called the Princess.

And through the turbulence of the last two days he remembered something that Tom Parker had mentioned on his whistle-stop tour of the island—Ned's Beach, where he could feed the fish. He'd paid scant attention at the time—it had made no sense—and yet, here he was now.

It was crazy. This was seriously the most ridiculous thing he'd ever done. The most pointless. But he dipped his hand into the fish food, scattering it all around him. The water erupted in a fevered flapping rush of silver and scales as open mouths fought for the food. Fish buffeted his shins, their bodies sleek and surprisingly warm, swept back and forth by the tide, swept up in the fight for the food.

It was like nothing he'd ever experienced. It was unimaginable. It was almost like the fish had been so well trained that they were waiting for bare legs to appear so they could rush into shore and be first for the feed.

He scattered another handful, and then another, entertained by the feeding frenzy and reminded of another day, long ago, when he and Sophia had celebrated the end of their university studies by taking a holiday in the United Kingdom. They'd hired a camper-van and criss-crossed the country. They'd stopped at St Ives, in Cornwall, treating themselves to cod and chips from a takeaway near the harbour. Sampling the local cuisine. Playing at being locals. They'd sat by the harbour wall and tried to eat their fish before the diving gulls could fly over their shoulder and pluck their meal from their hands. Competitive and determined, the gulls seemed to work in tag teams, one distracting you, the next taking advantage of an outflung arm bearing treasure.

It was a contest to see who would prevail—the humans or the birds. In the end, it was more of a draw. The gulls had won some points, but the best bit was when Theo and Sophia tossed the rest of their chips skywards and watched as the gulls engaged in a chip war with each other, any hint of cooperation or tag-teaming thrown asunder, the sky over them filled with the raucous flapping creatures.

They'd laughed so much. And when they found the signs afterwards requesting visitors not to feed the gulls, they'd realised their tourist faux pas and laughed even more. It had been one of the best days of their holiday.

Feeding these fish was a similar experience—except apparently here feeding the wildlife was allowed. Even actively encouraged.

The fish danced and darted around his shins, fighting for the food, fighting for supremacy, and it was so mad, so out of his world, that he did something that he couldn't remember. He felt it coming, bubbling up inside him, a feeling so unfamiliar that he didn't at first recognise what it was. Until delight erupted from his mouth in a bubble of laughter.

How she heard over the wind whipping around them, he didn't know. 'Do you see?' the Princess yelled over the wind. 'Isn't it fabulous?'

Theo couldn't deny it. And yet, as he scattered the fish food into the water, it wasn't just fabulous, it felt cathartic.

It was therapy. Laughing at the antics of the fish. Letting go.

It was—*fun*.

A fish nibbled one of his toes, taking a chunk of skin out of it. 'Ouch,' he said, but he was laughing, and when he looked up, he saw her watching him, and he stilled.

Her eyes glittered. 'You see. This island is magic.'

And in spite of himself, Theo was starting to believe it.

CHAPTER ELEVEN

THEO WAS CONFLICTED as he prepared for dinner. Isabella had requested for their last night on the island, that they book a table at the restaurant where she had worked. Still acting, or so she could say goodbye to the crew she'd worked with, the crew that had given her a chance and made her welcome.

He wasn't crazy about the idea. He didn't want the Princess exposed to the public eye any more than she already had been, but he wasn't a monster. And after today's excursions, he had to admit his attitude towards the Princess was changing.

She was much more of a surprise package than he'd been led to believe. Sure, she was young and naive, she was a twenty-five-year-old innocent Princess, and yet she'd proved herself so much more than that. She shown she had street smarts by evading recovery for so long—nobody had expected that.

She was no poseur; she had a natural way about her that belied her royal heritage. And if she hungered for the throne, there was a complete absence of evidence for that. Could she hide a yearning for the throne that well? No. Surely if she was planning some kind of coup against her brother, to take the throne in his place, she'd want to be working inside the institution that was the palace of Rubanestein, and not in some far-flung island half a world away—where internet was thready at best and totally absent at worst.

Hardly the place to plot a coup.

Perhaps most surprisingly, she was fun to be with. Sure, she could be annoying and problematic and too much in his face, like today when she'd sidled too close to him for his liking at the museum, but today had been fun. He'd forgotten about fun. He'd left fun by the wayside when Sophia had gone.

He'd had no place for fun.

But today the Princess had reminded him of the simple pleasure of fun. The simple pleasure of laughter. And that was no small deal.

No. The more Theo reflected on the case, the more he learned about the Princess, the less sense the Prince's reason for wanting Isabella back in Rubanestein made. Was Rafael more worried about her safety out in the big world without security and so over-egged the pudding? That was possible, especially if he were the bullying kind of character the Princess had claimed. A runaway royal lacking security was always going to be fodder for every nefarious group out there. The Prince hadn't needed to add to the story by claiming it was an act of rebellion by the Princess for not acceding to the throne herself.

All he'd had to say was that he was worried for her safety, exposed and alone in the big bad world. Theo would have believed that. Anybody would have believed that. Because the Princess was in danger. She might have been lucky or clever until now, but sooner or later her luck would run out and the other people interested in finding her would.

But none of that explained why she had run.

Her story that her brother had sold his own sister in exchange for the funds to pay his gambling debts was so far-fetched. He knew people were capable of evil deeds, he'd be out of a job if they weren't, but this was a prince, the ruler of his principality—and to sell his own sister, to marry her off to one of his cronies as if she were no more than a piece of his property, was so heinous—was it any wonder he had trouble accepting her claims?

Then again—why had she run? If it wasn't for that, what was it?

He ran his hand through his hair. The Princess—this entire case—and the extended time spent together because of this damned cyclone—were messing with his head. And today's fish feeding excursion was not helping.

It had broken too many barriers. He'd let his game down. He didn't do fun. He didn't want to do fun. Not with anyone. Least of all with her. Of course she would want to sway him. But she was a job. A rescue.

He just had to keep reminding himself of that.

Isabella showered and changed into a sundress for dinner at the café, knowing that time was short and that she was running out of options. Theo had advised her that the airport would reopen tomorrow, and that they would be on the first flight to Sydney. So that left her with just one night to convince Theo that he shouldn't drag her back to Rubanestein.

She took a deep breath. They'd had a good day today visiting the museum and Ned's Beach. They'd had a fun day. Even Theo couldn't deny that. She was hoping that Theo's attitude towards her might be softening, and that he might see her as less problem rescue and more as a woman.

He was starting to feel something for her, she could tell from the way that she caught him looking at her, but as yet there was no indication that he was not intending to carry through his mission.

It was frustrating and there was so little time left. She sensed that he was starting to see her not as a mere rescue, but as a person. A woman. He was softening to her. So, yes, her clumsy attempt that first night when she'd sneaked into his room had ultimately failed. But then, last night he'd been the one to kiss her.

What a kiss.

And today, he'd enjoyed their time at Ned's Beach. Theo couldn't fake that. She'd got the impression that Theo faked nothing. What you saw was what you got.

Isabella checked her reflection as she looked in the mirror. She'd twisted her hair into a messy bun with tendrils coiling around her face, and tonight she'd even added a touch of make-up, circling her eyes with a smoky kohl, adding a hint of blush and a smear of gloss to her lips.

She took another deep fortifying breath.

There was one chance left. *Tonight.*

One night to put Plan A into practice.

Seducing Theo. Getting him to admit that she meant more to him than any other rescue. Getting him to admit that he cared about her enough to not want to simply hand her over to her brother. Surely, if he made love to her, he would rethink his plans?

And if he didn't—well, if he didn't, and he still insisted on delivering her back to her ever-loving brother— she still would have a memory to look back on in the long, loveless years ahead.

One way or another, she needed Plan A to work. Otherwise she'd have to resort to Plan B. She hadn't got this far without having a backup plan.

Plan B was way less fun but could prove just as effective. Make a scene at the airport on their departure. Find security and plead for help. Accuse Theo of kidnapping and trafficking her and maybe worse. Making sure that he was the object of the authorities' attention. Her own ID borrowing would no doubt be an issue when that came out, but if it delayed the legal process, that was good. That worked for her.

But she didn't want to have to resort to Plan B. She didn't want to throw Theo to the wolves. She knew how the media worked. They would tear him apart based on a false accusation.

Ordinarily she hated women who made false accusations. It brought all women down, minimising genuine grievances. But right now, when she was desperate, what other choice did she have?

So, Plan A was it. She just had to pray that it worked.

'It's time,' she heard Theo call from downstairs. She bounded down the stairs and met Theo at the front door. He looked her up and down and for a moment he appeared dumbstruck. And then he said, 'You look amazing.' Had his voice gone down an octave? Whatever, the sound seemed to vibrate into her bones.

'Thank you,' she said, her eyes drinking him in. He

was wearing suit pants and a crisp white shirt that clung to his torso in the best possible way. Even better, the shirt was unbuttoned at the neck exposing a triangle of olive skin dusted with black hairs. 'So do you.'

They remained there for moments, seconds, before he seemed to remember that they were supposed to be leaving. He cleared his throat. 'We should go,' he said.

The minutes it took them to drive the slow route to the restaurant no longer felt like a penalty. Instead, it felt delicious. Isabella's senses were on high alert. Today they'd broken the barrier between hunter and hunted. Today they'd found common ground.

Happy ground.

And now, her senses buzzed at his proximity, at his clean masculine scent. She would be happy if this ride never ended. Except there was the anticipation of the after, and the prospect of that was even more delicious. And after today, after witnessing his joy at one of the island's simple pleasures, after witnessing Theo unwinding, there was a chance it might even work.

She sucked in a breath, heavily laden with the heat and scent of Theo. Was he wearing after-shave or was it his own signature scent that wove its way into and beguiled her senses?

And curiosity powered her conversation. 'What's the name of the after-shave you're wearing?' Because if she never met him again, she wanted to be able to buy it and be reminded of his scent and this time in her life.

'I'm not wearing after-shave.'

Damn. So much for buying a bottle. But she found a smile. 'I like it.'

'I said I'm not wearing any.'

'I heard.'

She sensed his head swivel towards her. She just kept smiling and turned her head out her window.

Around them, the palm trees swayed, while the waves crashed into the coral reefs surrounding the lagoon, the background music of the island restored to normal settings now the cyclone was moving away. Isabella had fallen asleep to the island's music night after night. She knew she would never forget this sound.

She turned back to him. 'You're so lucky the cyclone closed the airport.'

'Am I?'

'Of course. How else would you have seen anything of the island. But now, at least you've seen some of the sights.'

He grunted as he pulled into the restaurant's car park. 'I consider myself blessed in that case.'

She smiled to herself. He didn't sound it. It was fun teasing him.

The head waiter showed them to their table—table thirty—at the back of the restaurant.

'What are the chances?' Isabella said as she sat down.

'I requested it,' he told her as he pulled out his chair, 'Just to ensure you couldn't easily be spotted by any walk-ins.'

Isabella screwed up her face. 'Your job seems to suck all the joy out of life. Are you ever able to relax?'

'Yes,' he said. 'Between jobs.'

'I thought you'd relaxed today.'

'There were moments,' he said.

'You were happy,' she insisted. 'I saw it. You can't deny it. It was fun. How long is it since you last had fun like that?'

* * *

Theo didn't want to think about it. His mind was on to-morrow. He didn't want to be reminded of that day in St Ives, when he and Sophia had broken the local pro-tocol and flung chips into the sky and set off world war three—or the *gull war*, as they'd named it. He hadn't wanted to be reminded of it. It somehow felt disloyal that he'd had fun with another woman. *This woman.*

He'd never wanted any other woman. But getting in-volved with this woman would break all the rules. Per-sonal and professional.

'A while,' he simply said.

'That's so sad.'

Her expression looked sad, but the Princess was so upbeat. What was going on? She'd been almost flirty in the car. And yet tomorrow she knew that he would be taking her back to Rubanestein. Surely, she should be fearful. Apprehensive.

Instead, she seemed almost gleeful. What was that about?

Unless this entire adventure of hers had been a fraud, an adventure of her making, and now she was relieved that the game was over, and she was glad to be going home.

For Theo, who'd rescued people who'd wanted to be rescued, who'd wanted to go home, her constant flip-flopping made no sense.

Except, he had to admit to his own flip-flopping. His take on the Princess seemed to change at every turn. She was supposed to be innocent and naive. She'd proved her-self to be anything but. She was supposed to be a woman who hungered for the crown, and who'd turned her platinum hair, her crowning glory, into a crown of colours, and shown not one iota of interest in wanting to be the leader of Rubanestein or in inciting some rebellion. On the contrary, she seemed to be happy living half a world away and having nothing to do with her homeland.

Theo tried to pull it all together as Millie delivered menus to their table, trying to pretend she wasn't intrigued at them being together. Her brother's story made little sense. Her story made less. But maybe, just maybe her story was right. What if her story was right? It was bizarre and so far out there that it seemed impossible, but what if she'd been telling the truth all this time?

Millie arrived to take their drink orders. There was more she wanted to say, Theo could tell, seeing the questions so clearly swimming in her eyes, but she said nothing, merely taking their orders. Sparkling water for the table, and a glass of pinot noir for Isabella.

'Do you want to tell me about it,' she asked, 'about that other time you felt so happy?'

'Not really,' he said, turning his attention to the menu. 'Now, what do you like to order?'

'We had a good day today,' she said, looking over the menu.

'Haven't we already discussed this? Why are you bringing that up again?'

'Because we did.'

He could find no way to disagree. 'It was fine.'

'You laughed,' she said. 'You had a good time.'

'It has been known to happen.'

'I bet, not for a long time.'

He said nothing but his silence spoke volumes.

'So,' he said. 'What would you like to order?'

* * *

'I think I'm going to have the steak,' Isabella said, closing her menu, 'medium rare. With the garlic roasted chats on the side.'

Theo grunted.

'Something wrong?' she said.

'No,' he said, closing his menu as Millie returned to their table bearing their drinks.

'Are you ready to order now?'

'Two scotch fillets, medium rare, with side of the roasted chats for two. And if you could,' he added, 'we'd appreciate it if you would move us up the order.'

Millie nodded and smiled. 'I can do that,' she said, and promptly disappeared into the kitchen. Isabella surveyed him through her lashes as she took a sip of her wine. Was that the reason for his grump, that she had chosen the exact same meal as him? Was he annoyed that they had even this one more thing in common than the way they took their coffee?

Theo was baffling to her. An insufferable mix of kidnapper and yet self-proclaimed protector—allegedly. Every time the door opened, his head swivelled, checking who was going in or out.

'You're making me nervous.'

'What?'

She waved an arm towards the door. 'All that constant head swivelling. Who are you expecting?'

'I'm protecting your safety. If you don't appreciate that, then I'm sorry.'

'If you're interested in protecting my safety, you wouldn't be delivering me back to Rubanestein like a trussed-up chicken. You'd be helping me get away and stay away. You'd be protecting me from my brother.'

'You keep saying that.'

'Because it's true! And you are going to feel like one stupid jackass when you realise it.'

Theo said nothing. Simply swivelled his neck when the door opened again. Isabella turned to look, too. Theo stared at the entrants, a couple with three children, and turned back, apparently immediately discounting them as a threat.

'Gosh,' she said. 'Do nefarious agents not use children for cover any more? Times have certainly changed in the world of subterfuge.'

'Give it up, Princess. That family was in the museum when we visited today. If they'd wanted to make a move on you, they could easily have followed us to Ned's Beach and snatched you there.'

'Oh.' Isabella vaguely remembered other visitors being in the shop when they'd visited but hadn't taken in the details.

'Yes. "Oh." You see, I do know something about my business.'

Isabella felt the rebuke like a smack. Even though she no doubt deserved it, she regretted her words. She was supposed to be trying to make Theo feel closer to her. To make him warm to her. To make him see that she was more than just another recovery.

Thankfully Millie arrived then, delivering their meals. 'Two steaks, medium rare,' she said, placing the sizzling plates on the table in front of them, 'with a side of garlic roasted chats.' She held her tray vertically in front of her. 'Is there anything else I can get for you? Are you all right for drinks.'

'Thank you,' Theo said. 'Nothing else.'

The steak was perfect. Izzy's knife sliced through the tender steak as if it were butter, the roasted potatoes crispy garlic perfection. She'd ordered thinking she needed to keep her energy for the night ahead. But her appetite had disappeared, and she barely finished half her meal.

It was impossible to eat while she felt her frustration mounting. This was crunch time. Tomorrow hung over her neck like a noose. She had to make one of her plans work. But she had to get him talking. She had to get him warming to her.

Theo was not acting like someone who wanted to talk or warm to her. It was like he'd recognised that he'd let his guard down at Ned's Beach today, and that he'd revealed too much of himself and so was trying to shut himself down. She took a deep breath. What she needed was a different angle. Less combative.

'So, the plan for tomorrow is that we take the flight to Sydney,' she started, twirling her glass of pinot noir, 'and then we board your private jet to Rubanestein?'

'That's the plan,' he confirmed.

'Still the plan?'

'Still the plan, Princess. The plan hasn't changed. The plan has always been set in concrete.'

'I knew that,' she said on a sigh, because Isabella couldn't help but be dismayed. She'd hoped Theo's attitude to her was softening, but despite her arguments and her pleas, he was resolute in returning her to the place she least wanted to be. 'But is there any chance you might possibly relent? Maybe give me more of a chance to prove what's in store for me when you return me home?'

'Why would I do that? You've already had two days to convince me, and you haven't yet.'

She lifted her glass, went to take a sip and put it down again out of frustration. 'I hate that you don't believe me. I think I hate you right now. Excuse me, but I need to go to the bathroom.'

'Don't try to sneak out a window, Princess. We've already done that. It's getting old.'

She stood up and walked away. What chance did she have to win Theo over to her side? How was she going to seduce him? Her Plan A was a confection. A faint hope.

How could she possibly seduce a man who was more like a robot? Unemotional. Wedded to his purpose. Oblivious to reason. His brief glimmer today of a human hidden beneath that shell of concrete completely and utterly snuffed out.

How did anyone, let alone her, seduce a man made of stone?

It was impossible.

Millie caught her arm on her way back. 'What's going on?' she whispered. 'Are you sure you don't need help? I can call the policeman now, if you want.'

Izzy shook her head, running a hand through her hair. 'It's a long and boring story, Millie. You really don't want to hear it.'

'You're wrong there, but I guess if you can't tell me, you can't tell me. And if it's an easier question, let me know how you're placed for shifts next week.'

'I wish, but it looks like I'll be leaving the island tomorrow if the airport reopens, so tonight looks like it's goodbye. One day I hope to be able to explain it all.' *Although she very much wondered when that might be possible.* Izzy wrapped her fingers around Millie's hand. 'Meanwhile, thank you so much for your friendship. It's been fun working with you.'

Millie frowned. 'Are you sure it's all okay between you and—' she glanced over Izzy's shoulder '—him.'

'It's, uh, complicated. Trust me, and maybe one day I can tell you.'

'I want that,' Millie said. 'I want to know all is good in your world.' The two quickly embraced. 'And know that whenever you come back, you'll always have a job here.'

Izzy felt tears pricking her eyes. 'Thank you. That means the world to me.'

Izzy was almost back to their table when Millie caught up. 'Oh, I almost forgot to tell you.'

'Tell me what?'

'Apparently two guys came in today at lunch when I was off duty. It was weird because they said they were looking for someone called Erin but they showed a photo that looked a bit like you.'

Ice flowed through Izzy's veins, fear stiffening her spine. 'What were they told?'

'That they didn't recognise the photo. But apparently it really looked like you, Izzy. Apparently, now you've washed the colour from your hair, she looked like a dead ringer for you.' Millie frowned. 'Are they looking for you? Are you sure you're not in trouble?'

'What's going on?'

Neither Isabella nor Millie had noticed that Theo had

joined them. Millie started, as if afraid to confront Theo directly.

'Someone was asking questions earlier today,' Izzy said. 'Someone looking for a blonde woman who looks just like me.'

'But how did they get here?' Theo asked. 'The airport is closed.'

'Apparently a private launch arrived this morning, mooring at the supply boat dock. People noticed it because it was so crazy to attempt making the crossing from the mainland in that weather. Nobody had seen either of them before. They must have been from the boat.'

'Can you describe them?'

'Only from what I heard. They were broad-shouldered and wearing suits. They didn't look like tourists.'

Theo cursed. 'Get your things,' he told the Princess. 'We have to go.'

'Should I call the police?' Millie asked.

'No. No police.' He dropped a stack of bills on the table. 'That should take care of the bill and a tip for you.' He nodded. 'Thank you. In case anyone asks, we weren't here.'

Millie was still chewing her lip as Izzy squeezed her arm. 'Don't worry. I'll be fine.'

Izzy wished she believed her own words as Theo headed the car for the apartment. He was angry, she could tell, no doubt at the accursed weather for delaying their departure, no doubt at knowing that whoever else was tracking her was getting close.

But his anger in no way matched hers.

'Well played, Theo. You were the one to demand I wash the colour from my hair.'

'What of it?'

'And so people noticed a resemblance. It's only because the waiters were suspicious that they pleaded ignorance. But who else have they—whoever they are—flashed that photo to and who aren't suspicious enough to want to protect my privacy? You did that. You made me instantly recognisable by making me wash the colour from my hair.'

'You don't know that.' But he did know for a fact that he'd flashed the photo of a smiling blonde princess to Tom Parker, and it had stirred his memories, even though her hair had been coloured all the colours of the rainbow.

'You do! You were so incensed that I'd dared colour my hair and sully my Princess roots that you made me wash it out. You were so sure that we'd be on a plane the next day that you didn't think for a moment that maybe it was better to keep my disguise in place until we were on our way?'

He growled, a low and guttural sound emanating from his throat.

'Is that all you've got to say, bounty hunter?'

'Anyone might have recognised you in that photo anyway, colour or no colour.'

'Might have. But you ensured it was a certainty. Thanks for protecting me. I think I was actually doing better by myself.'

She flung her head back against the headrest. Hell. What was she going to do now? Her backup plan to make a scene at the airport was looking increasingly more perilous. If she made a scene, if there were agents on the island looking for her, and one of them was no doubt stationed at the airport watching every departure—it wouldn't just be security who noticed.

Was that preferable to trusting Theo?

CHAPTER TWELVE

THE PRINCESS WAS RIGHT. It was Theo's fault. He'd known people had been on his tail ever since he'd taken over the case, it had only ever been a matter of time before they would discover the identity swap the Princess had made in Sydney that he'd discovered himself. It followed that it would only be a matter of time before they'd follow him here, to Lord Howe Island.

Theo had led them straight to her.

Thank god he'd found the Princess first, but now that the storm had prevented them leaving the island, they were sitting ducks. No wonder she was angry. The only silver lining now was that she might actually believe him, that others were actively searching for her. But he wasn't about to throw that in her face. This wasn't a point scoring exercise. This was serious.

'I'm so sorry,' he told her on their way back to the apartment. 'I'm so sorry I've brought this down on you.'

'You should be,' she said, her teeth troubling her bottom lip. Her options for escape were shrinking. Hope evaporating with it.

Escaping Theo was one thing, having plans to change his mind or elude him, was one thing, but knowing there were others also after her complicated any hopes of escape.

The ride back to the apartment was no way a repeat of their ride to the restaurant. Now the slow ride was painful. A painful reminder of all the things that remained unresolved between them. Now their drive seemed never-ending as her brain tried to work a solution.

How was she supposed to seduce him when anger fired her blood and filled her veins? What point would there be even trying if he was so determined to bring her back to her former life and a loveless future, whatever she tried? And if she couldn't, how was she ever going to succeed at making a scene at the airport and getting away. The airport had only a handful of flights in or out. It was the first place the agents would have staked out.

What the hell was she going to do?

At long last they arrived at their accommodation and Isabella sprang out of the car the moment he pulled up. 'I hate this,' she said, storming down the hallway. 'You have stolen my freedom from me. You've entrapped me and given me no choice. Are you happy about that?'

'What?' he said, tossing car keys down on a hall table.

'What do you think? Now that there are people some-where on the island after me, I have no choice but to re-turn to Rubanestein with you.'

'You were always going to be returned to your home, Princess. Either that or be caught by rogue actors. You just didn't accept it. Thank your lucky stars it was me who found you first.'

She tossed her head. 'Thank you? For putting me in this situation? For insisting on dragging me back to

Rubanestein when it is the last place I want to go? I don't think so.'

'So what of your other choices?'

She kicked up her chin. 'I had plans.'

He snorted. 'Well, good luck with those, Princess.'

'I was doing fine until you showed up. Maybe you should just leave me here, to deal with whoever else it is looking for me. Surely my fate couldn't be any worse than being returned to Rubanestein.'

He shook his head. 'Please, Princess, your brother is trying to save you from danger.'

'And what about the danger to me being sent home? My brother doesn't give a damn about me. He believes I'm his chattel—nothing more than a bargaining chip he can auction off to the highest bidder.'

'Stop it. I don't want to hear it. You're a princess. How did you expect your life to unfold?'

'I expected to marry for love!' She furiously paced the length of the living room and then back again. 'Didn't I tell you? Weren't you listening? My father knew that I would never accede to the throne. He knew that. I knew that. So, he promised me that even though I wouldn't take the crown, I would be able to marry for love. I wanted to marry for love and that was his solemn promise to me. What is so wrong with the concept of marrying for love?

'What is wrong with saving myself for the man of my dreams. So how do you think I felt, once I discovered that I was going to be deprived of any of that, that I was going to be married off to some revolting crony of my brother's in order to pay off his gambling debts, and that I didn't have a say in any of it—why are you surprised that I ran? Why are you so surprised that I don't want to go back? Don't you think I had good reason?'

He pinched the bridge of his nose with his fingers. 'And wanting to marry for love is the reason why you threw yourself at every surfer and barista going during your little adventure? Because you wanted to save yourself for your one true love?'

Her jaw jutted. The golden lights in her eyes glowed hot. 'What else was there to save myself for? What was the alternative? My choice, or my brother's, someone determined to decide for me?'

He ran a hand through his hair. 'This is getting old, Princess. You have to take this seriously. You need to pack. There's no point us trying to find somewhere else to stay tonight. The last place we want to be is on the roads when the top speed limit is twenty-five kilometres an hour when there are people actively searching for you. We'll hunker down here. I promise I won't sleep. Nobody will get to you.'

'But you're here. And you're just as bad as them.'

'Princess—'

'Don't "princess" me! I'm clearly worth nothing in your eyes. No more than one more so-called success story to attach to your CV. Yet another notch on your gun. You disregard everything I say while you drink up every word my silver-tongued brother feeds you as if it's the gospel truth. Do you hate me that much that you could deliver me back into the living hell my brother has in store for me? Do you just plan to hand me back, take your thirty pieces of silver and then wash your hands of me, job done?'

She made a sound of desperation. Half gasp, half sob.

Her lips pressed tightly together and she put her fingers over her mouth. But it was too late to hide her raw emotions. He could see the tears springing from her eyes even as she squeezed her eyes shut, her shoulders juddering as she gave in to her feelings.

And Theo was torn between his duty and her distress. Torn between admiration that a naive princess had eluded discovery for so long, and frustration that she refused to accept what her discovery meant. Torn between respect for the fight in this pint-sized princess, and desire. Desire that had been building from the moment Theo had captured her in his arms and felt the heat triggered between them and smelled her citrusy scent.

Because she was wrong about one thing. She wasn't worth nothing in his eyes. She was worth so much more than that. But she was still a princess. He had no right to have feelings for her. He wasn't entitled to feel anything for her. She was a case. She was a rescue.

But she was also a woman. A woman in pain. And her coming undone broke something inside him.

'Princess,' he beseeched, taking a step closer. 'Please?'

Her eyelids scrunched even tighter. Her mouth screwed and twisted under her fingers. There was the briefest shake of her head before she turned away on another sob and fled towards the stairs.

'Princess,' he called, chasing after her. 'Isabella.'

He caught up with her before the stairs, catching her by one arm, the momentum swinging her around. She crashed into him, and immediately raised her fists, pummelling his chest. 'I hate you,' she said, 'I hate you.'

He got that. He understood why. He understood why she needed to take her frustrations out on him.

For a moment he let her beat his chest with her fists. She was so impassioned. So fiery and fierce. 'It's okay, Princess,' he said, holding her by both shoulders now as her fists continued to rain down on him with no sign of relenting. 'Let it out. Let it all out.'

The Princess didn't need encouragement. She continued to take out her rage against him, but her fists were beating slower now, her sobs less frequent, until her head lobbed down against his chest, soaking his shirt with her warm tears as her shoulders continued to shudder under his hands. Now her fingers were curled, clutching the fabric of his shirt, clinging to him.

She wasn't acting. She was broken, deflated, her spirit shattered. The spirit he'd admired, even grudgingly, ever since he'd taken on this case and found the Princess to be more than just a naive twenty-five-year-old royal.

'You're right, Princess. I deserved that. I'm sorry.' He dipped his head down to hers. It was a mere impulse that his lips brushed her hair, kissing her softly on the head. Nothing more. An act of consolation, that was all it was intended to be. Sympathy. Empathy. The tiniest of kisses as he drank in her so familiar citrus scent. And it occurred to him that he would miss that when he'd returned her home.

Damn. He would miss more than that. He would miss this woman, with all the frustrations that came with her. More than that, with all the temptations that came with her.

Her shoulders stilled as slowly she raised her head, lifting her tear-streaked face to his. Her eyes were red-rimmed and puffy from her tears, her cheeks hot where they'd rested against his chest, her lips still pressed tightly together. But in spite of that, she was still one of the two most beautiful women he'd ever met.

And this woman was here.

Now.

It wasn't a conscious decision. It wasn't any kind of decision at all. It was more an imperative. 'Princess,' he said, as his head dipped lower. 'Isabella.'

Her breath hitched. Her eyes widened. Her pink lips parted on a gasp. And it was all the encouragement he needed, any glimmer of doubt that he was doing the wrong thing disappeared in less than a puff of smoke. His hands moved from her shoulders to skim her back and wrap her in his embrace.

His lips met hers. Softly at first, drinking in the sweetness of her mouth, tasting the salt of her tears, making him want more of her. Making him want all of her. He wanted to experience all her flavours, the sweetness and the salt, the spice and the umami.

She took her sweet time, almost as if she didn't trust him, thinking that he might once again realise he'd overstepped a mark and that he would pull away like he had done last night. He didn't break the kiss to assure her that wouldn't happen. He sought to reassure her with his mouth and lips moving over hers, with his hands and arms pressing her closer to him. Maybe it was all of those things, or maybe it was his tongue, plundering the hot depths of her mouth, enticing hers into the dance, because suddenly, like a switch had gone off inside her, she kissed him back with a fervour that matched his own, her hands framing his face, pulling him deeper into a kiss that rocked his soul and that told him one thing—he hadn't been wrong to kiss her last night. The only question in his head as her mouth opened hotly to his was why it had taken him so long to realise?

His hands skimmed down her sundress, relishing the feel of tight, toned skin beneath, cupping her buttocks and squeezing their ripeness. She groaned in his mouth as she arched her back, pressing her breasts and the hardened bullet points into his chest. Breasts that didn't require any bra. Breasts he ached to release from their bodice. Breasts that had driven him crazy ever since he'd seen her in first her pyjamas and then that tiny bikini that had tied him up in knots.

And suddenly he couldn't wait to see them anymore. He lifted her to his waist. She went with him, wrapping her legs around his torso, the action pulling her skirt up high, baring her legs. He groaned. He only had two hands, and two hands were nowhere near enough when he had this much going on around him. Smooth, slim legs, the sweet curve of a buttock. Everywhere his hands glided was filled with reward. But standing up was not where he wanted her now. He backed her into his bedroom, dropped to his knees by the bed, and folded her gently down onto it.

She looked shocked that he'd let her go, her eyes wild with surprise, desire and need. Until she realised where she'd been laid. A brief smile touched her lips. 'Theo,' she said, in that beguiling accent she had and that held an inherent promise that banished sense from his head and punched a hole in his heart at the same time.

He reefed off his shirt, got to his feet and shucked off shoes and pants. His erection sprang free and he witnessed the Princess's eyes widen, looking hungrily at him.

'I think I'm overdressed,' she said, her voice husky. Shaky. Uncertain.

'I'll take care of that,' he said, slipping off her shoes before sliding his hands up her legs, hooking fingers into her underwear, and tugging it slowly down. There was nothing for it then but for her sundress. He skimmed it up her thighs, then her waist, and slipped it over her breasts. She gasped, as if feeling the rush of cool air against her nipples, but lifted her head so he could fling the garment away.

And then he looked down at her, drinking her in with his eyes. 'Perfection,' he said, taking the time to drink in her petite hourglass figure. His cock bucked in agreement.

She held out her hands. 'Please,' she said, as if uncomfortable with his gaze. 'Please.' Okay, so she was relatively new to this, and maybe her lovers hadn't taken the time to show their full appreciation. But then he wasn't inclined to take his time now, not when she was so eager.

And it had been so long.

He didn't want to think about how long. That time ceased to exist. He just wanted to live in this moment. He wanted to bury himself in her. Here. Now.

Bury himself in Isabella.

Except… *Protection.* He wasn't carrying. He'd given that up years ago. He'd given up thinking he'd ever need it again. But he was sure he'd seen something discreetly positioned in the side table. He reefed open a drawer. *Bingo.* He pulled out a foil packet, tore it open with his teeth and sheathed himself.

Next time they could take their time, he told himself, as he lowered himself over her perfect body. Because he knew with the certainty of a man who had found a second chance at paradise that there would be a next time.

He kissed his way up her legs while she squirmed on the bed, her breath coming in heady gasps and mewls of surprise and delight as his lips made their way north, over her jutting hip bones and the slightest swell of her belly to her ribs. He kissed one tight bud of a nipple and then the other, before he circled it with his tongue, and drew her breast into his mouth. Her spine arched, forcing her breasts higher to meet him—to welcome the attentions of his hot mouth and to turn his attentions to her second breast.

His cock bucked, aching for completion, but it was no hardship filling his mouth with her second breast. Her skin tasted delicious. Of warmth and honey and that increasingly familiar citrus scent that suited her so well. That he would never forget.

And all the time her hands were in his hair, her nails raking his skull as she clung to him as he made his oral onslaught. When he found her mouth, she drank him in like she'd been trapped in the desert and he was the oasis, the water source, the life giver.

Little had he realised that it was she who was the life giver. Little by little, day by day, she was giving him back his life.

Laughter. Joy.

Hope.

Resting over her on one arm, he swept the other down the side of her torso to her hips, where his hand found her mound, his fingers separating her, sliding into the folds between her thighs. He was rewarded by her heat and slickness and the promise of magic.

His erection juddered against her belly at the knowledge. She shuddered and shifted one arm, and the next thing he knew was that she had taken hold of him with one hand, encircling him with her fingers and taking him to the limits of his control.

She groaned, a sound of need that fed and built his own. 'Please,' she cried, urgent and insistent and almost like she was pleading for her life. 'Please!'

He was already primed to go off. Her touch only notched that up. And he knew that there was no more time. There was no more waiting.

Next time, he thought in what was left of his remaining brain cells, next time, they could take their time. Next time they could explore each other's bodies at length, tease each other until they were both begging for release.

Next time.

But next time could wait. This time was now.

He positioned one knee between hers and she opened for him. Opened herself up for him. He found her core, found his place. He still wanted to take it as slow as he could. Wanted to preserve this perfect moment where his mouth was on hers, his arms cradling her head, her arms at his shoulders, clinging on, anxiously waiting.

The breathless moment before. The moment of anticipation where time stood still.

Suddenly he couldn't wait a moment longer. His cock bucked one more time and his hips moved with it, pushing him, driving him into her. Except, in spite of her slickness that met his glans, there was no easy glide, instead he met resistance that made no sense. But then, it had been a while, he was rusty at this. And the resistance just made his thrusts work harder.

Until something gave, there was a sound, and he was inside her, her walls wrapping tightly around him in the most intimate of embraces.

Bliss.

Theo wanted to howl with success. He let himself feel the perfection of being enclosed by tight flesh that wrapped around him, cocooning him, before he was withdrawing, his hips moving to their own score. Not all the way, this connection was too important to lose. Before he plunged into her again. And only then did the sound he'd heard make some kind of sense. A cry, coupled with the resistance he'd felt. He didn't want it to register. He wanted to blot it out, he wanted to deny it, refute it, his body already on a trajectory that he could no longer stop or wanted to, but one that he sensed could ruin his life—and hers—forever.

But it was too late, and right now there were more important things to worry about.

She cried out, calling his name, her muscles tightening around him, urging him on, desperate to hold on to him when he withdrew, welcoming him when he plunged ever deeper. Until he emptied himself in one final juddering thrust. Her cries told him of her own climax as her whole body shuddered around him with her own orgasm.

His bliss was short-lived, as the whole horror of what he'd just done registered. And post-coital bliss turned to self-hate in an insta-second. There was no time for wrapping her in his arms and cuddling her next to him. No time for breathy kisses and warm shared words as their bodies hummed down from their heights. Instead, Theo pulled out of her, sat up on the side of the bed, rubbing his jaw with one hand before he headed for the bathroom, wanting to rid himself of the evidence of his actions as if he could so easily wipe out the truth of it. He returned to the bedroom to pull on his underwear, before turning to look at her.

'Why didn't you tell me?'

The Princess looked still shell-shocked, like she'd been thoroughly made love to as she had, her hair mussed, her features in glorious post-coital disarray, and that didn't help matters at all. That just made him angrier.

'Tell you what?' she asked breathlessly.

'What do you think? That you were a virgin!'

Her eyes flickered between opened and closed. 'Oh, wasn't that in the dossier you were given?'

'Actually, it was. But since then, you've had however many flings with some surfer dude and a barista and who knows however many else. Isn't that what you said?'

She sighed, pulling the covers up over her, but not before he saw a telltale smear of blood on the sheets.

'Did I ever say that I'd slept with any of them?' She raised herself up on one elbow and looked at him disingenuously. 'I might have admitted to being tempted, but I never admitted to having sex with anyone, did I?'

It was worse than Theo had imagined. It was a horror story but a horror story of his own making. His rescue was a virgin—*had been a virgin*—and he'd been the one entrusted to return her home, but he'd been the one to deflower her. It was a nightmare.

'That was—um, nice,' the Princess said from the bed. 'Is there any chance we might try that again?'

'No! Was this one of your plans, then, Princess? To seduce me and try to convince me not to return you to your homeland?'

She blinked, looking sheepish. And he didn't need her to answer to know that he'd been played. That this had been her plan all along. To seduce him, to bend him to her will. A pity it wasn't going to work.

He pulled the bedcovers from her. 'Get out of my room. Pack your bag. And stop with the tears, because, like it or not, you're going home to Rubanestein tomorrow.'

He didn't wait for her response. He took himself to the bathroom, stepped into the shower. If he couldn't erase every memory of what had just happened, he could at least try to erase every possible scent of her from his body.

Forget thinking that the Princess might be telling him the truth. Forget thinking that she might have a case. She was a manipulator, pulling his strings any way she could. A sob story about her brother bartering her off. A sob story about him abusing her puppy. Forget feeling sorry for her, or that her brother was taking advantage of her. She'd just pulled the worst strings of all.

Her story was rubbish.

As a result, he was more determined than ever to deliver her back to her home. She would be someone else's problem then.

And they were welcome to her.

CHAPTER THIRTEEN

ISABELLA MADE HER WAY back to her bedroom trance-like, her clothes clutched in her arms. Theo had made love to her, worshipping every part of her body, and it had been spectacular. More spectacular than she could have ever imagined. There had been no time for her body to recover, she was still glowing, her senses still hypersensitive, the space between her thighs still humming.

And for once it almost didn't matter that he was still determined to return her to Rubanestein. Not after tonight. Tonight, she'd discovered the wonder of what making love to a man you wanted to make love to was like. This is what she'd always wanted, to know what it was like to make love to a man that meant something to you.

Okay, so this wasn't a man who was going to marry her, but her dream of marrying for love was already in shreds, and if she had to take a second option, she'd settle for making love to Theo. She'd never have come up with Plan A if she hadn't been attracted to him. If she hadn't felt the heat of their connection. If she hadn't felt the magnetism between them.

And whatever happened in the future, she wanted to file that memory away, knowing that this one time she had actually had sex with someone she wanted to. And it had been glorious. And Theo had seemed to be enjoying it too, if she hadn't been mistaken. He'd been so eager for her. So hungry.

Until the moment he'd realised.

A shame. She'd wanted Theo to be on her side. An ally. She'd so hoped he would be on her side. He was a protector. She needed protection.

But there was no more protection for her. Theo was more determined now that he would deliver her back to Rubanestein and would walk away, leaving her to her fate. And maybe he had cause for walking away, but she would never forget him.

She'd railed against him from the very start, fighting against his heavy-handed insistence that he was taking her home against her will. But at the same time, she'd been fighting against an attraction to him that had been so unwanted and unexpected and yet so stealthy that it had managed to worm its way into her senses. Or maybe it was him, his voice, his scent, his body heat that had wormed its way into her senses?

That would do it.

Maybe that's what had done it.

Maybe that's why she felt conflicted, and why she couldn't deny feeling something for him even while she resented him for being so insistent on taking her back to her brother. Because she did feel something for him. She didn't have the wherewithal or the brain power to ana-lyse that right now. Her mind was too heavily engaged in replaying over and over what had happened tonight. The good bit. The first bit, before he realised and sent her packing.

She laid her head on her pillow knowing she wasn't

even going to try to sleep, because her memories of being made love to by Theo, of being reminded of his touch, of his hot mouth, of the feeling of being filled by him, were far more compelling.

Who needed sleep when your body had been awakened to the pleasures of the flesh?

The next morning the winds had eased, the cloud cover evaporating. The traces of the cyclone had moved away, the twin peaks of Mt Lidgbird and Gower now clearly visible under an ever increasingly sunny sky.

But while the weather had moderated, the relations between the two occupants in the apartment hadn't. The mood in the kitchen was frosty. Words hadn't been exchanged since last night's lovemaking. Any hope Isabella had that Theo might have relented in the night, and that his thoughts would soften towards her after what they'd shared turned to nothing. Theo almost refused to acknowledge her.

There were no offerings of making coffee or tea or toast from either of them. It was every man and woman for themselves. Bags were duly packed and waiting at the front door.

It was frustration that forced Isabella to speak after Theo pointedly refused to acknowledge her presence. 'How exactly are we supposed to evade whoever is after us? They must know what times the flights come in and out.'

He glanced at her, his eyes cold, as if he'd wished she hadn't spoken. 'Exactly why we're going out on a private flight I've organised. If they're watching the airport for scheduled departures, hopefully we'll catch them off guard and be gone before they notice.' And then he turned away to check whatever news had just burped into his phone.

'Why are you being so cold to me?'

'What?' he said, wanting to focus instead on the update he'd received from one of his agents.

'If I remember correctly, we made love last night. Do you even remember making love to me?'

'What if I do?'

'You weren't cold to me then. Instead, you were hot—'

'Forget it,' he snapped. 'Last night was a mistake, Princess. Last night didn't happen. And I would seriously advise you to wipe it from your memory.'

'Oh, but it did happen, and I'm not convinced I could actually forget. I'm not sure I want to.'

He turned away. 'It was a mistake.'

'It was the most amazing experience of my life.'

'I'm happy for you, Princess.'

'But I wasn't a princess to you last night, was I, Theo. I was Isabella, pure and simple. I was a woman.'

'In reality you were a princess then, and you're a princess now.'

She shook her head. 'Do you want to know why it was the most amazing experience of my life?'

'Not really. I don't think we need to do this. I really don't want to hear it.'

'I think you do. I thought we both enjoyed a connection that had been growing, and that culminated last night in the most amazing experience.'

'Last night was the only "connection" we had. End of story.'

'No. We shared something more impactful than that.

I know you did. I felt it. And I doubt I will ever experience sex like that again, making love to someone that I wanted to.'

'It was sex, Princess,' he said dismissively. 'It was a primal need. It was a scratch following an itch. Nothing more. So don't go reading anything romantic into it.'

'You say that, but I'm grateful to you. I'm so glad you gave me that experience, that you were my first. So that I know how good making love can be. So that I can remember. In all the rubbish days and nights ahead.'

He shook his head. 'I wish you'd stop lying to me. You led me to believe you were an innocent.'

'I never told you that. That's what you'd been told. All I said was that I'd met other men.'

'You lied by omission!'

'I never lied, by omission or by any other means. If you assumed something, that's all down to you. You believed what you wanted to believe. You'd been informed in your dossier on me that I was a virgin. I mentioned meeting Mateo and Luke and how hot they were, and your mind goes there. That was never me. That was you, filling in gaps, the way you wanted to fill them. I told you from the start, I wanted to marry for love.'

He arched an eyebrow at her. 'So what was last night about? If not trying to seduce me around to your cause so I might look more benevolently upon you. So I might be more inclined to take your side and be less willing to return you to Rubanestein?'

She looked down. 'That was my plan. True.'

'You admit it. Bravo.'

'Except,' she added, licking her lips, 'I think there's something we're both missing.'

He sighed. 'And what would that be?'

'Last night was amazing. You can't deny that. Last night wasn't an accident. Last night was mutual. You wanted to make love to me as much as I wanted to make love to you.'

'Princess…'

'No, listen to me. Whatever plan I might have to make you relent and to bend you to my will—and I admit that was my hope—what was your plan? Why did you make love to me?'

Because he couldn't help it. He couldn't prevent himself. Because this pint-sized princess had somehow wormed her way into his senses, and he couldn't resist her any longer.

But he could hardly admit that. 'It was a mistake,' he said, needing to shut this conversation down. 'Why can't you simply accept that?'

Why was he even arguing with her? What was the point? After he'd made some necessary calls making arrangements for the next morning, he'd spent the night trying to work out where he'd made the fatal mistake of crossing not just a line, but an entire eight-lane expressway. He'd beaten himself up about it until his psyche was bruised, his mind bloodied, and yet still, there was a part of him that couldn't forget how good she'd felt in his arms.

And he hated himself all the more for the fact it wasn't clear-cut. That he was conflicted. That he couldn't simply put her out of his mind. That part of him was drawn to her even when he knew she'd played him every way until Sunday.

He wished he could tear that part of him down, rip it

away and toss it asunder. He had a job to do. He had to focus. She was a princess. A rescue he had to get home. Nothing more.

She couldn't be more.

It was impossible.

The arrival of Tom Parker's van in the driveway was a relief. Finally, they would be on their way.

Tom loaded the bags into the back of the van. 'Unusual to be leaving this early for the airport,' he said. 'The flight's not until eleven.'

'Private flight,' Theo said. 'Beating the rush of all the people backed up wanting to get off the island,' he added by way of explanations. 'But that's just between us. I'd appreciate it if you didn't pass it on.'

'Got you,' Tom said, conspiratorially tapping the side of his nose with one fingertip, as Isabella emerged from the apartment. Tom smiled a greeting at her. 'I'm just glad you managed to find your friend. I hope you had a happy birthday, Izzy.'

Theo thought back to that first day, when he'd first shown that picture of the Princess to Tom and asked if he'd seen her, leading to him finding her that night at the café.

Theo clapped his hand on the other man's shoulder, 'You helped me no end,' he said, before holding that same hand out to the Princess, throwing her a warning expression at the same time. 'You got a big surprise when I found you, Izzy, didn't you,' he said.

She regarded him warily, her eye twitching at his informality, but still she took Theo's hand. 'A bit of an understatement,' she said, adding a small laugh. 'But thank you, yes, it was most definitely a surprise.'

'I'm glad,' said the beaming Tom. 'The island prides itself for being a magical space. I'm glad the magic worked for you both.'

Theo pressed his lips together as they climbed into the car. There had been moments of something resembling magic, but they had been few and far between, most of his time here marred by frustration borne by both lack of sleep and exasperation. Ultimately any magic the island could bestow had been wasted on them. Okay, so it would be pointless denying that there was an attraction between them, but no amount of island magic could change the facts of their situation. Bodyguard and rescue. Commoner and Princess. He was a professional first and foremost. He'd always been going to bring the Princess home.

What had happened last night was an aberration. Nothing more.

The airport car park was quiet, too early for scheduled arrivals and departures. The windsock stirred half-heartedly on its pole, the fury of the storm moved on. Theo made sure to check out who was there before he gave the all clear, Tom whisking their baggage from the car and into the tiny terminal even as a small plane could be seen approaching the runway.

'That's us,' Theo said.

The plane landed, taxiing to a stop just outside the terminal. Propellers stopped. Stairs lowered. And within a few minutes their luggage was stowed and they were boarded, Tom farewelled and the plane was already taxiing for take-off.

Then the small plane lifted off and the car and anyone chasing after her were left far behind them.

And Theo sighed, closed his eyes thinking, with a two-hour flight to Sydney, and nowhere for the Princess to run, that maybe, finally, he might be able to get some sleep.

He closed his eyes. Drifting with the small plane's rumbling into that blessed sleep state.

Soon, he thought. Soon—*finally*—he would be rid of her.

CHAPTER FOURTEEN

TURBULENCE WAS SOMETHING Izzy was used to. She'd flown over European mountain ranges, she'd landed in helicopters in high winds over ski fields and into deep valleys, but as Theo's private jet approached Rubanestein airspace, the turbulence in the air was nothing compared to the turbulence going on in her mind.

Their escape from Lord Howe Island had been smooth and effective. Their transfers at Sydney's airport had been slick, through private lanes where they were treated as VIPs, clearing customs and immigration. It wasn't just that she was a princess, Isabella could tell. It was some kind of clout that Theo had. Almost as if he was known and recognised.

She'd considered trying her abandoned Plan B, to make a scene at the island's airport on their departure to alert security. She'd considered trying it in Sydney but abandoned the idea just as quickly. Theo seemed to have some sort of cachet with the authorities. Like he was the one more likely to be trusted.

And then, knowing that there were people after her and so close behind, did she really want to risk being restrained in Australia?

It was the worst of all worlds. What choice did she have?

It wasn't long before they were welcomed onto Theo's private jet. The plane was luxury personified. A sleek jet with cream-coloured leather seats, panelled timber walls and a lush, carpeted floor, the kind of flooring she'd noticed on her recent travels that you didn't find in the commercial cattle class she'd used to hide her travels.

Beyond the stylish lounge, dining and office seating, she'd been shown a luxurious bedroom and bathroom she was welcome to use.

At any other time, in any circumstance, Isabella would be happy to take such a flight. But her relief at getting away was rapidly giving way to a growing dread. Of being returned to Rubanestein, her brother and his plans for her.

There was no escaping his plans for her.

And the closer the plane got to Rubanestein, the more her dread rose, like bile in her throat.

'We'll be landing in thirty minutes,' the flight attendant told her. 'Is there anything I can get you before we start our descent?'

She shook her head. 'No.'

She knew the instant the plane started its descent. Izzy felt it in her gut, and felt all hope go south with it.

She turned to the man in the seat opposite, the man who had said not a word to her this flight. 'You won't tell my brother, will you?' she pleaded. 'You won't tell him?'

He looked up. 'Tell the Prince what? That we fed the fish at Ned's Beach? Something else?'

'That I tried to seduce you. And then that you made love to me.' Her eyes pleaded with him.

He sighed. 'Do you really think I want to tell the Prince that?'

'No. Maybe not straight away. But it could get out. Another way. In the press or on social media. You know the sort of thing. *"A close source says that while the Princess was in Australia she was uninhibited. Desperate, and begging for sex."* Do you realise how much that might compromise me in the future?'

'Oh Princess. Do you really think me capable of that?'

'For money? If someone offered you enough?'

He shook his head. 'You don't know me at all, do you?'

She thought she did. At least a little. But they'd had such little time together, what did she really know of him? Except for how hot he was and how good he'd felt inside her.

'But you're doing this for money, aren't you? Returning me to Rubanestein for money?'

He slow blinked. 'Yes, I get paid for returning you. But that's not my motivation.'

She considered that for a moment. 'Oh, so you're just the good guy. The saviour. Doing good for good's sake. How noble of you.'

He sighed. 'You're angry with me. Because I'm bringing you home, or for some other reason?'

'You made love to me,' she said.

'I did,' he admitted. 'And I told you it was a mistake. I told you I was sorry about that.'

Her lips pursed. 'But I'm not sorry. I'll never be sorry for that.'

She turned away before he could see the truth in her words, before he could witness the single tear that escaped from each eye. She'd treasure the memory of that night forever, the memory of feeling wanted. Even loved. The way she'd always wanted to be loved.

By a man she'd set out to seduce to make him protect her.

A man who'd turned into someone she believed she could love, and yet a man who'd betrayed her. She wanted to hate him for delivering her back to her brother's clutches.

She wanted to hate him.

But all she felt was sorrow.

CHAPTER FIFTEEN

THE JET WAS on final approach to Rubanestein's one and only international airport when Theo's phone buzzed. He found the message as their plane taxied to the private aviation area. It was a relief to have a diversion from the Princess's latest outburst. 'There's a banquet at the palace tonight and I've been invited,' Theo told the Princess. 'Apparently the Prince is celebrating your return. It seems you've been missed.'

'Lovely,' she said, her expression deadpan. 'Just what I wanted, to have to endure another few hours in your presence.'

Theo was equally unimpressed. He'd expected to bring the Princess to the palace, collect a cheque, turn around and fly home. But given the pilots and crew had earned a break after their arrival, Theo would be going nowhere. Apparently, the Prince wanted to thank him personally. It was a polite gesture. Very civilised.

What Theo wasn't surprised about was the Princess's response. He'd expected her to be dismissive. She'd become more and more sullen the closer they got to Rubanestein. Because of course, she hadn't got her way. She'd been delivered back to Rubanestein, to her own country. To where her duty lay. But most of all, out of harm's way. What was her problem? She'd had her flings. She'd had her freedom flight. Whatever grievances she had with her younger brother, why couldn't she accept that her life should be one of duty in the country of her birth?

And he didn't feel guilty in the least, because she'd deceived him. If she had told him the truth from the start that she had been a virgin, he would never have touched her. She knew that. Instead, she'd flaunted tales of her times with Luke and Mateo and hinted about others and made him believe that her innocence was no longer an issue.

She'd tricked him, tricked him into betraying his trust. Tricked him into betraying his duty of protection for her.

So he couldn't blame her entirely for that, because she'd always been forbidden to him, virgin or no. He never should have touched her. And not just because she'd been forbidden. But damn, now he didn't think he'd be able to get the taste and feel of her out of his head.

How did one erase one of the most sublime moments of your life? One of the most life-changing? She'd moved like liquid silk in his arms, so responsive to his every touch, so reactive to his seeking mouth and tongue.

Liquid silk.

Hot and fluid. She'd moved like a ballerina in the bed. Graceful and lithe, as she'd wrapped him in her limbs and welcomed him into her body.

And it had been wondrous. Magical. A revelation. Until he'd felt that unexpected resistance.

But by then it was too late and his next lunge swept away any and all hint of resistance. Leading up to that, he'd heard her whimpers of need, he'd heard her jagged breathing, sounds that had fed into his own building need, but when he'd heard her cry out as he'd lunged into her, he'd realised what he'd done.

Fool.

He was supposed to be a rescuer. A protector. A bodyguard.

If there was a bodyguard how-to book, Rule Number One would have been, don't fall for your rescue. Don't engage in some kind of reverse Stockholm Syndrome, where you fell for the person that you were rescuing, no matter how attractive and sexually alluring and infuriating they were.

He'd broken the first rule in the book.

And broken it big time.

And the Princess was worried Theo would tell the Prince that he'd deflowered his sister? Not a chance.

The plane came to a halt. The door was opened, the steps lowered just as a cavalcade of dark-windowed SUVs drove alongside, a red carpet rolled out for them to disembark, before whisking them away to the palace, a fairy-tale castle atop the clifftop complete with towers topped with slated turrets and bearing the flags of the principality.

The Princess was shown to her wing of the palace while Theo was shown into a suite of rooms, in which he saw a king-sized bed laid out with a formal outfit he was apparently expected to wear tonight, along with an entire wardrobe from swimmers and gym wear to casual wear, everything he might need for his stay.

It seemed his every need had been anticipated.

It made a kind of sense, he thought, because none

of the luggage he had brought contained anything formal enough for a banquet. It was a kind and thoughtful gesture.

He checked the labels. The sizes were spot on. Somebody had clearly done their homework.

He took advantage of the pool with a long swim. With lap after lap he felt the tension easing from his muscles, his body releasing the tension that had been accumulating these last few days. It was relief to be here and have the Princess safely returned to her country. It would be more of a relief when he had departed, closed this case and moved on. This dinner was an inconvenience, a timing issue, nothing more.

He refused to think about what had happened between him and the Princess—a mistake—but for now, it was good to know she was back where she belonged and the sooner he could get away, the better. The sooner these unnerving feelings would disappear. It was proximity making him feel this way. He needed to be away. Divorced from the drama of a runaway royal and whatever angst she was feeling.

He was dressing for dinner when the report he'd been waiting for lobbed into his inbox—the deep dive into Prince Rafael's gambling proclivities, if they indeed existed as the Princess claimed. Quickly he opened it, scanning the contents.

Interesting.

More than interesting.

Damning.

Because apparently the Prince was neither a fan of the horses nor one to frequent the casinos that graced Rubanestein's shores, confirming what Theo already understood. But there was shade, his researcher had found.

Something that Theo hadn't known. Something that nobody had known. Details were sketchy, disguised under layers of cybersecurity, but there were indications the Prince may have had a penchant for bitcoin and other cryptocurrencies and had taken to crypto gambling in an effort to try to leverage his gains. A high-risk strategy where the chance of losses and accumulating debt was also high.

Gambling.

Theo thought about all the times the Princess had claimed that her brother had racked up gambling debts. Gambling with cryptocurrency on online unregulated casinos—there was a potential recipe for disaster.

And Theo's spidey senses quivered on high alert.

Because, if the Princess hadn't been lying about the gambling? What else might be true?

Theo was directed to his seat of honour, a seat next to a bejewelled throne where Prince Rafael would sit. On the other side of the empty seat, a wiry man sat down, grinning and bowing his head to Theo, introducing himself as Count Lorenzo di Stasio. Theo nodded and smiled in acknowledgement.

'We are beholden to you for returning our Princess,' he said.

'Thank you,' Theo said. 'But I was just doing my job.'

'And you did it well.'

They were interrupted by the blare of trumpets as Prince Rafael stood at the door, in the uniform of Rubanestein, a gold sash over his chest, and a beautiful woman on his arm. The Prince's consort, Theo guessed, though he'd missed that detail in the dossier. She was dressed in a strapless gown of pink lace, a long scarf of the same fabric wound around her neck, her blonde hair in an updo, curvy tendrils framing her face topped off with a diamond-encrusted tiara.

Everyone at the table stood as the couple came closer. Wait? *Blonde hair?*

He looked closer. Her eyes were smoky with kohl, her lips were painted the same shade as her dress. But it was her. This was the Princess Isabella, in full royal regalia. He was so used to her dressed in beach wear, casual summery island wear that he almost hadn't recognised her.

And Theo had to acknowledge, she was magnificent.

She hesitated as she regarded the room. Before she took a seat beside the man opposite who took her hand and kissed the back of it while the Prince moved to his place at the head of the table.

She looked up at Theo then, just a momentary glance—a glare—before she swallowed and then looked away.

And Theo's spidey senses went into overdrive.

Everyone sat, and the Prince turned to Theo. 'It is good to meet you at last, Theo Mylonakos. Do you find your accommodations comfortable?' he quietly inquired.

'Exceedingly so, Prince Rafael, I thank you for extending me your hospitality.'

'What else could I do?' he said, his arms raised either side, 'But welcome the man who has brought my errant sister home. You have done our principality a great service.'

Then he turned to the room. 'It is a beautiful day,' he said, his voice booming in the vast banqueting room. 'I have called this banquet in honour of my sister and our

Princess Isabella being returned to us and our family reunited. It is a day for celebration. It is a day for celebrating family.

'And I have to thank my firm friend, Theo Mylonakos, for making it possible. This man, above all odds, found our adventure-seeking princess and brought her home.'

Applause met his words, the guests universal in their nods and smiles and the enthusiasm of their applause.

Applause that didn't sit well with him when Theo was in more doubt that he'd done the wrong thing, and he deserved censure rather than applause.

'But right now, there is a feast to be enjoyed. Please,' the Prince said, benevolently spreading his arms out wide. 'Enjoy.'

A bevy of waiters delivered platters of food to the table. Fluffy flatbreads and dips, salads and other offerings. There was spit-roasted lamb, lemon-roasted chicken and potatoes along with baked fish and eggplants roasted in a garlic yoghurt sauce. Along with of course, the paella for which the coast was famous.

Theo sampled it all. To the left there sat the Prince, to his right there sat the head of the security services who made polite conversation about Theo's work.

Music interludes smoothed the spaces between the conversation, but all the while he was watching what he said while keeping an eye on what Isabella was doing.

She barely made a move towards the food. Despite her make-up, she looked pale, her eyes wary. The man next to her—the Count—seemed to dominate her, directing her choices to what he permitted her to eat. He was middle-aged, Theo guessed. Probably in his fifties. And Theo's gut churned.

Minute by minute as the meal progressed, the sick feeling—the fear—inside Theo grew. Theo tried to engage with the Princess a few times, but the Count soon shut down the conversation. Theo wanted to shut him down. But he couldn't do that. But still his senses crawled. And Theo hated it.

The dinner was winding to an end, the Prince calling for a toast.

Theo imagined that it would be a toast to him, for bringing his sister home. But no. It was a toast to his sister's upcoming marriage, to the Count Lorenzo di Stasio, a wedding that would take place tomorrow.

And after he'd dropped that thunderclap, he turned to Theo, and said, 'Of course, you must be here for the wedding. I insist. The union that you've made possible.'

The Count smiled and bowed while the Princess shrank in her seat, looking more afraid than he'd ever seen her.

The Princess hadn't been lying.

Why that should have smacked into his head with the force it did made no sense. Hadn't he been suspicious of the Prince's flimsy story? Hadn't he been partial to believing hers, of her brother's bullying, of his cruelty? At least until they'd made love and he'd discovered that she'd omitted to tell him that she was still a virgin and he'd wanted to punish her.

'Congratulations,' Theo said through clenched teeth, recovering enough to raise a glass. 'Of course, I'll be here to witness the happy event. To the happy couple.'

Everyone joined in with the toast. Everyone he noticed, apart from Isabella, who skewered him with daggers from her hazel eyes.

And he knew he deserved every one of them. He'd failed to believe her. He'd let her down. And so much of her marriage tomorrow was of his doing. He'd delivered her up to this. Because he was angry with her. Because she'd been a virgin and she'd led him to believe otherwise. Any sympathy for the Princess had evaporated on the spot. He was taking her home. Instead, he'd brought her to the gates of hell of a forced marriage.

Her head was turned towards the table, but her eyes were upturned to his and he saw them glaring at him. Hating him.

And he knew he deserved it.

But what did she expect him to say? How could he object? How could he protest? He was in Rubanestein. Even if he wanted to, he couldn't simply snatch up the Princess and run. They would be caught before they reached the airport, his jet already impounded.

No, he needed another way. His mind scrabbled to find one. He could not leave the Princess to marry this wiry, aged Count, who did not deserve to sit next to her, let alone share her bed.

It came to him as the banquet wound down, desserts served and consumed. It was clear that Prince Rafael was a man motivated by money. It was also clear during the banquet that he was a man fond of his wine.

The banquet at an end, the Prince invited Theo, the Count and the Princess to repair to the salon for port and cigars. The men sprawled in armchairs, while Isabella sat apart, her posture stiffly erect, looking more and more downcast.

Theo accepted the cigar, also accepting a glass of port

while the other men employed cigar cutters to remove the cap before lightly toasting the end.

The Prince watched on, as if in no hurry to light his own cigar. 'I have to hand it to you, Theo, we thought your business had failed in your quest to find the Princess. The agents I sent out to follow you admitted that they were no match.'

'You sent out your own agents?'

'Of course, I did. They thought they had you two days ago. It was the closest they'd got. Maybe if the storm had lasted longer on the island, they would have caught up with you? But maybe they served their purpose in hurrying you home.'

Theo swallowed. Those two agents on the island that night were Rafael's agents? Those two agents who'd set tempers flaring between Theo and the Princess, which had dominoed into them making love only to discover the Princess was a virgin, turning his anger upon her, when she'd never deserved it.

His throat was dry. But it was neither port nor a cigar he needed. It was to spell out the truth.

'Your sister is a lucky woman, Prince Rafael,' Theo said, 'to find such a worthy husband. How did their engagement come about?'

He caught the arrows the Princess fired at him from her eyes.

The Prince snorted. 'Simple,' he said. 'Count Lorenzo offered me the most money to take her off my hands.'

Theo laughed along with the Prince. 'Genius,' he said, raising his glass to him. The Prince, as he'd expected, drained his, clicking his fingers for a refill.

'So, how much is the Count paying you?'

The Prince smirked. The Count laughed and inter-jected, 'One hundred million dollars. US currency.'

Isabella interjected, clearly aghast. 'You are that much in debt from your gambling?'

'No, silly woman—but I need to be left with some play money after the dust has settled. Surely even you can appreciate that?'

'Women,' Theo said dismissively. 'They have no con-cept of the price or value of anything.'

'You see that, Theo? You are indeed my brother.' The pair clinked glasses. 'You understand how the world works.'

Theo fully understood how this man worked. 'One hundred million dollars,' Theo said, nodding. 'That's not bad.'

'It's excellent. And you made it happen by bringing her home.'

The Count was laughing. 'I told you we appreciated your assistance.'

Theo could see the Princess fuming. He could al-most see the waves of heat rising from her. Right now, he imagined her painting him as much of a bastard as her brother.

Hang in there, he wanted to say, but he could say nothing.

'But one hundred million US dollars?' Theo mused. 'Is it anywhere near enough for such a prize? The Prin-cess is of good child-bearing age, and to her credit, not entirely unattractive.'

The Prince spluttered. 'What do you mean? Is it enough? It's one hundred million US dollars.'

'But what if you could do better?'

The Count jumped to his feet. 'We have a deal!'

The Prince waved his hand at the Count. 'Sit down, sit down. Tell me, Theo, my brother, how could I do better? It's the best offer I've had.'

'What if someone offered you double?'

Isabella's head snapped up. Suddenly she was interested in what was going on.

'Who is this someone?'

Theo let the silence settle. He took a sip of the mellow wine and this time he enjoyed it. 'Me.'

Isabella gasped, standing up. The Count grabbed her arm, pulling her back down. The Count started spluttering. 'We had a deal. We *have* a deal! The wedding is tomorrow. Prince Rafael, you can't change your mind now.'

'Shut up,' the Prince snapped at the Count. Before scratching his chin and turning back to Theo. 'Double, you say? Two hundred million US dollars.'

'Exactly. And I'll waive my recovery fee in addition.'

The Prince sat up. 'Well, that shines an entirely different light on things.'

'I object!' said the Count. 'We made a deal. The wedding is planned for tomorrow.'

'Ah, true,' said the Prince, stroking his chin. 'We had a deal. And it would be wrong to not acknowledge that. So I'm giving you an opportunity. Can you match Theo's offer? No—can you better it? Because there's already a better offer on the table.' He turned to address the Count directly. 'You need to offer more.'

The Count visibly swallowed. 'Prince Rafael, this is so unfair.'

'Can you?'

The Count's voice was getting weaker. 'We had a deal...'

'I see. So you can't. Then I have no choice. Theo Mylonakos, in exchange for two hundred million US dollars, the Princess Isabella is yours.'

CHAPTER SIXTEEN

It took some twenty-four hours before the money transfers had been successfully concluded and they were on the plane and out of Rubanestein airspace. Finally, Theo allowed himself space to breathe.

His nerves had been on a knife-edge ever since that dinner invitation. Ever since finding that report in his inbox, ever since seeing the Princess sat beside an older man that she'd clearly not wanted to have anything to do with, his sickening spidey senses had told him that the Princess had not been lying.

And that Theo had personally delivered her. He might as well have wrapped her up in a sparkly gift box wrapped with a big red bow.

But now the jet and they were safely away. Theo unclicked his safety belt and stood. He needed to walk. He needed to find a way to burn off this nervous energy that had surrounded him for too long.

The Princess he could see was sleeping in her seat. She'd fallen asleep the moment they'd taken off.

God knows what the last few days had been like for her. Afraid of her impending arrival back in Rubanestein. Afraid of the impending nuptials her brother had planned. Afraid the Prince might change his mind again, after he'd agreed to take Theo's money in place of the Count's.

She'd had more at stake than he'd ever had, and he knew how nervous he'd been this last twenty-four hours.

He hated himself for delivering her lock, stock and barrel into a marriage she wanted no part of. A marriage she'd warned him was going to happen if he returned her to Rubanestein. And yet, he hadn't believed her. Even though he'd been swayed, wanting to believe her, she'd then lied to him and that had turned him against her.

He was wrong.

So wrong.

He just hoped that one day, she might forgive him.

An hour later the Princess stirred. Refreshments were served. 'How are you feeling?' he asked.

'Better,' she said, cradling a cup of tea. 'Relieved.' Then she looked up at him. 'I haven't had a chance to properly thank you yet.'

'Don't thank me. I did you no favours. I should have believed you. There were times I wanted to, but it seemed so mad, so unbelievable that your brother would want to do that to you.'

She smiled. 'My not so darling brother. I'm sorry to leave Rubanestein and its people, but I'm not sorry to leave him.' She shuddered. 'And the Count. You know, I actually believed you were going along with the Prince at the banquet. Do you know how much I hated you in that moment?'

'I knew. The look in your eyes made that crystal-clear.'

She shook her head. 'And then you pulled a rabbit out

of a hat. Two hundred million US dollars. Where did you even get that kind of money?'

'The rescue business pays well—so long as you can rescue people, that is. I make it a point of rescuing people.'

'You save people.'

'I try to. I made it my job. And when there were too many cases or one person, I expanded my business. Nobody realised how many cases there were. Missing babies. Sons and daughters gone missing. Partners disappeared. Princesses disappearing off the face of the earth.'

She looked up at him. 'Did you have many princesses disappearing off the face of the earth?'

He shook his head. 'Only one, and she proved to be the case to end all cases. She evaded all and every attempt to track her down. We're going to have to rewrite the book about runaway royals after this.'

'You found me,' she said.

'You didn't make it easy.'

She laughed and smiled up at him, 'I'll take that as a compliment. But I'm so glad it was you who found me.' But where did that leave them? Where did they go from here?

'So, what happens now?' she asked, licking her lips. 'I owe you for what you've rescued me from, and you bought me, so do you own me? What do you expect me to do?'

He shook his head. 'Nothing. I don't own you. You're a free agent. I bought you your freedom, not your life, and certainly not your servitude. And after what I did, you owe me nothing. Accept your freedom as my apology. You now have all the freedom you always wanted.'

She nodded. Freedom. It sounded good. It sounded like exactly what she'd been seeking.

Except...

On a deeper level it was also disappointing. She paused, searching for the right words, knowing this moment was make or break. 'What if I don't want to be a free agent?'

'What?'

The Princess licked her lips. 'What if I'd prefer to spend my life with someone else?'

The growl rumbled deep and dark from the back of his throat. 'You're still thinking about Mateo or Luke or whoever else there was?'

She smiled. 'I'm touched you remember their names.'

He shook his head. 'Look, I don't care who it is. I don't want to know. You're free to be with whomever you like.'

'Except I don't know if it's possible. I don't know if this person feels the same way.' She tilted her head. 'Would you agree to take me on, for better, for worse, for richer or poorer, in sickness and in health?'

'Wait. What? Are you proposing to me?'

She swallowed. 'I told you once before that my dream was to marry the man that I loved. Are you the man I'm going to marry? Are you going to make my dream come true?'

'You don't marry someone because of a dream.'

'No. You marry someone because you love them, and you want to spend the rest of your life with them.'

It took Theo but a moment for her words to register. He understood now why he had such a visceral reaction when the Count had pawed the Princess at the banquet.

He understood what had been staring him in the face ever since he'd taken her to his bed on Lord Howe Island. He understood what had been building ever since she'd tumbled into his arms from her bedroom window and what had driven him crazy every time she was close. Every time she was near.

He'd fallen in love with someone he should never have fallen in love with.

He'd fallen in love with Isabella, but now he could finally admit it.

He pulled Isabella from her seat and into his arms. 'Princess,' he said, his mouth hovering over hers, 'Isabella, I love you so much.' Their lips met, and Theo felt something powerful crack open inside him, the stone walls that had surrounded his heart since he'd lost Sophia, and now his heart was open. Open to welcome Isabella.

But kisses were not enough. He needed to show her just how much he loved her. Needed to finish off what they had only just started at. He swept up her legs and carried her to the bedroom, closing the door behind him with his foot.

He laid her on the bed so tenderly, like she was made of porcelain, fragile and delicate. He knew she was far from that; she had an inner strength that belied her age and upbringing. She was clever and resourceful. Bold and beautiful. But to him, in this moment, she was the most precious creature in the world.

Looking back, Isabella couldn't quite remember the order of things, who shed their clothes first, whether it had been her to tug off his shirt and pants or whether she'd been too busy in the tangle of arms and limbs and seeking hands tearing her own clothes off. But then they'd both been naked and it was magical. Skin against skin. Lips and hot mouths against skin. Senses overloading. Need spiralling, until Isabella was spiralling with it, losing her mind, losing control.

When he entered her in one long thrust, this time he met no resistance, she felt no shock of pain. Instead, she welcomed him into her depths knowing that this man was the one she'd been waiting for her entire life. Knowing that he was the one. The only one.

He built momentum with each thrust, building the desperation, the madness consuming her, until with one final thrust he sent her over the edge, and she was flying, literally and figuratively into the sky.

He followed, juddering into her, rolling her climax into crested waves of paradise.

Afterwards they lay together panting, their shared breath fanning across the heated skin of their bodies. It was bliss to share this time together while their bodies hummed down from their peaks, a magical time that had been denied them last time.

He leaned over and kissed her on the forehead. 'I love you,' he whispered, smoothing back loose tendrils of her hair.

'Thank you,' she said. 'I love you too.' But his heartfelt words had brought tears to her eyes. She swiped the dampness away.

'You're crying?'

She sniffed. 'Happy tears,' she said. 'Happy because I'm with you.'

He kissed her. 'I think I must be the happiest man in the world to find love not just once, but twice.'

And because Theo had brought the subject up, Isabella felt emboldened to ask, 'How long were you married?'

'Six years.'

'No children?'

He shook his head and sighed, probably not even aware that he was stroking Isabella's hair. 'It didn't happen,' he said gruffly, 'not until it was too late.'

Isabella felt a wall of longing and pain behind the simple words he'd uttered, but she wasn't about to ask what he meant.

'What was she like?' she asked instead.

'Sophia had dark hair and even darker eyes. She was beautiful, inside and out. She was perfect.'

Isabella pressed her lips together. It was ridiculous to feel envious of a dead woman, but it was impossible not to. If Theo felt even a fraction of that emotion for her, she'd be happy. But Sophia had set the bar so impossibly high.

'How did you two meet?'

'At university in Athens. We studied economics and international relations together.'

Isabella nodded. She sensed there was a world more pain behind his tortured eyes and strained words.

She smoothed his brow with one hand, trying to ease whatever pain he was feeling—whatever pain he was remembering—and after a while, he sighed. 'She was the daughter of an international banker. She was kidnapped and held for ransom. The police bungled the recovery. She was killed when they stormed the building where they discovered they were keeping her.'

He sighed. 'The autopsy discovered she was pregnant.' He looked at her then, his eyes tortured, his brow twisted. 'She hadn't had a chance to tell me.'

'Oh my god, I'm so sorry.' She raised herself up on one elbow and looked down at him, her fingernails tracing through his chest hair, and there, in the depths of his dark eyes, she witnessed the extent of his loss. 'And that's why you do what you do?'

He pinched the bridge of his nose. 'That's when it started, but I think the seeds were planted years before when my younger sister drowned. We were at the beach together, caught in the same rip and though I tried, I couldn't reach her. I couldn't save her. I hated that I couldn't save her.

'And then, when Sophia was killed, I made a solemn vow to do my utmost to prevent anyone else suffering the same fate.'

'You can't be blamed for failing your sister.'

'I know.' He took one of her hands in his, and kissed the back of it. 'But it made me realise what loss felt like. Coupled with the loss of Sophia, it made me want to save others from that pain.'

'I get that,' she said.

He shook his head. 'Sophia was amazing. I was the boy from the country. I never knew what she saw in me.'

Isabella was in no doubt. 'I know what she saw,' she said. 'Sophia saw a man of honour. A strong man. A protector. A man who would fight for what was right. She saw that in you, I know. Because that's what I see in you. That's who you are.

'And that's who I know you to be. Because you saved me,' she said, 'from a life of bondage and enslavement in a marriage I never wanted nor could be happy in. I can never thank you enough.'

'No.' He raised himself up to push her down on her back. 'It is I who needs to thank you,' he said. 'I was stuck in a life of endless guilt for failing to save my sister and my wife and trying to make up for it every day since. I was stuck in a life chasing my tail and never catching it. And for forgetting about the simple things in life. Like what it felt like to have fun. You reminded me what fun was. You reminded me what it felt like to laugh. You reminded me what it felt like to love.'

He pressed his lips to hers. 'You saved me,' he said, before he kissed her thoroughly again. 'And I love you forever for it.'

Isabella was breathless by the time they paused for air. But there was one question she still needed to ask. 'By the way,' she said, 'you never answered me.'

'About what?'

'Will you marry me?'

'Do you want my answer in words, or deeds?'

'How long have we got before we land?'

He smiled, looking hungrily down at her. 'Hours and hours.'

She scrunched up her nose, wove her arms around his neck and pulled him down to her. 'I guess there's no harm trying deeds.'

He kissed her lightly on the lips. 'That's the right answer.'

EPILOGUE

Lord Howe Island's Ned's Beach had turned on its best weather. The sea shone cobalt blue under the sun, the waves softly rolling, the sea breeze softly tugging at hair and fluttering silken scarves.

The guests were gathered on the lawns that bordered the beach, waiting for the main event, while tourists paddled through the shallows, laughing and delighted at the feeding fish frenzy that ensued every time they scattered another handful of fish food.

Their focus was all upon the fish wars at their feet, until the car arrived with the bride on board and the whoops of those feeding fish quieted, as all eyes turned to the bridal party alighting from the car.

Tom Parker opened Isabella's door, and she stepped from the car, her veil immediately captured by the breeze, fluttering up behind her. She took a moment with her bridesmaid Millie to check each other's dresses and lipstick, before the two gathered their bouquets. Millie exchanged a hug with the bride before setting off towards the assembled guests. Once Millie reached the aisle, Tom Parker held out his arm for her. Isabella took a deep breath, steadying herself, before she inserted her arm through his, and they set off.

Isabella was so happy as she made her way towards the aisle, she felt like she was sure she must be glowing brighter than the sun. Smiling wasn't an option, it was an imperative. This was the culmination of everything— a life of believing that she would marry a man who she loved, then months and weeks of stress and uncertainty and the fear that her dream would be snatched away from her. Only to find love in the most unlikely of places. In the man who had intended to return her to her hellish future, until he stepped in at the last minute and rescued her.

And now she was marrying him on the island that had provided her with sanctuary, and where that love between them had sparked and grown. Tomorrow she and Theo would climb the heights of Mt Gower, the first day in the rest of their lives together, every day providing new heights.

Tom turned down the aisle, and Isabella saw the man who had claimed her heart standing before the simple altar. Theo. The man she loved. His mother and father looking on, beaming. For a second she paused, her heart skipping a beat. It was almost too much. It was unbelievable.

'All okay?' whispered Tom beside her.

She sniffed as she turned her face to his. 'Never better,' she said, small tears of happiness squeezing unbidden from her eyes. He smiled, giving her arm a reassuring squeeze, and they resumed their slow march down the aisle.

Theo waited at the altar. Never before had he felt so nervous. Sure, he'd done this once before, with Sophia, and that time had been magical. But he'd never expected to find love a second time. Life was never expected to be so kind. But life had served him up a second chance.

With Isabella.

He knew the moment she'd started down the aisle. He heard the guests' 'oohs' and 'ahs'. He'd told himself he wasn't going to look. He fully intended not to look but he couldn't help himself.

He couldn't wait. He couldn't stop himself from turning.

And at the sight that met his eyes, he was so glad he did. He saw Isabella heading down the aisle towards him. Towards their joint future together.

She was dressed in a gown, form-fitting and sleek, a halter neck exposing her perfect shoulders and arms, smiling at those she passed. She was a vision.

Perfection.

As if knowing he was looking, she looked up at him and as their eyes connected, a bolt of lightning coursed through him.

Moisture welled from his eyes. He had to twist his lips shut in an effort not to give a very un-man-like sob. Because happiness was so large a gift that he had been given. And because he knew, without a shadow of doubt, that this was supposed to happen. Their pairing was fate. Their pairing was destiny. This was the second chance he'd never believed he was entitled to, but which fate had decreed he was.

He watched her make her way towards him. He didn't mind the slow bridal march. He didn't care how long it took. Because before this day was over, he knew that they would be married, and that Isabella would be his wife.

She met him at the altar. 'You're so beautiful,' he said,

taking her free hand in both of his, overcome with the emotion of the moment.

'I love you,' she said.

'And I love you. You've given me back the light. You've given me laughter. You've given me love. More than that, you've given me hope. I can never thank you enough for that.'

She squeezed his hands and looked deep into his eyes. 'And you've given me freedom. To live the life I want. To love the man I want to love. You are that man. I love you, Theo. I will love you forever.'

The registrant waiting before them subtly coughed into his smile. 'Perhaps we might get this wedding started...?'

* * * * *

If you fell head over heels for Greek's Royal Runaway, *why not explore these other sensational stories from Trish Morey?*

Bartering Her Innocence
A Price Worth Paying?
Consequence of the Greek's Revenge
Prince's Virgin in Venice
After-Hours Proposal

Available now!

Get up to 4 Free Books!

We'll send you 2 free books from each series you try
PLUS a free Mystery Gift.

FREE Value Over **$25**

Both the **Harlequin Presents** and **Harlequin Medical Romance** series feature exciting stories of passion and drama.